That certain something

clare ashton

That Certain Something

Editor: Jayne Fereday
Cover: Fereday Design

Published by:

BREEZY TREE

ISBN: 978-1-499-33118-9

For Diana
who wasn't far from my mind

1

Pia walked around the edge of the quiet London square while affecting an air of nonchalance. She kicked out her boots and hummed a song but, underneath her arm, she kept a tight grip on her camera and long zoom lens. She peered over her sunglasses. No-one walked outside the tall Georgian terraces. No-one sat underneath the trees of the large private garden in the centre of Kensington Square. She wriggled her shoulders underneath her rucksack and, with one last peek around, attempted a nimble jump over the black railings into the garden.

She landed with a gentle thud on the grass and to a tearing sound from her rear.

'Bugger.'

Left behind on a railing spike was the frayed back pocket of her jeans. She twisted round trying to check her bottom. It remained stubbornly out of sight and she spun round on the spot, rather like a dog chasing its own tail. She patted the previous location of her pocket and her warm hand found a cool patch of naked bottom.

'Damn it.'

Two pigeons startled in the trees above and she cursed herself for shouting. They grappled with a swinging branch in their panic, flapping against leaves, and a small droplet of liquid green plummeted to the floor.

Pia dodged the super-speed dropping and giggled as she squinted up. 'Sorry for scaring the crap out of you, pigeons,' she whispered.

She was about to launch up the nearest tree when she caught sight of a woman entering the square. Pia squinted through the bushes and hoped she hadn't been spied. The woman tilted her head to speak into her mobile. Long honey blonde hair fell around her face and she curled it away behind an ear with elegant fingers. Her dress was smart, but not in a corporate way. A tailored shape, cream, sleeveless to show slim arms and short enough to give a hint of long shapely legs. She carried a tablet in a case by her side and Pia was intrigued by the sophisticated lady.

'Give me an hour sweetie,' the woman said.

The melodious, well-spoken voice reached Pia. She watched, entranced by the soothing low tones that flowed through her.

'Sorry. I can't make it any sooner, not in rush hour.' The mellifluous sound made Pia tingle inside.

'Of course I'm looking forward to it.' The woman laughed, an alluring soft sound, and she stroked her fingers through her long hair. 'No I must admit, it's not my usual Friday night, but I'm hardly going to let you down.'

The woman's cheeks flushed in a smile that lit every inch of her face. It was a beautiful expression. She had high cheek bones and full lips. The curve of her jaw, the elegant line of her neck and the smooth rise of her chest were beguiling. Mesmerised, Pia was lost down her cleavage, when the woman turned on her heel and sauntered out of the square.

'Come on. Concentrate Benitez-Smith,' Pia said. She shook her head to break out of the hypnosis the woman had cast.

After another glance around, Pia slung the camera over her shoulder and hopped onto the bench at the base of a large plane tree. She started to climb and, after a mouthful of leaves and the odd snag on a twig, she settled herself astride a large branch with a good view of the tallest house in the terrace.

She leaned on her elbows and focussed her lens onto the four-storey town house. She zoomed in on the ground floor and scanned past the perfect white façade and glossy black door. She switched to manual focus to peer through the sash window into the house. A large kitchen and dining room swept back and generous gardens glowed green through the rear windows. No-one was in sight.

Pia lifted her lens to the first floor and was surprised to find it a grey blurry mass. It also moved. And it also made a noise. Pia peeked over her camera to find a peeved squirrel chattering and squeaking at the end of the branch. It dashed towards her, made an irritated noise and scurried back to turn and stare. If she could speak squirrel she would have guessed that it said something along the lines of: 'Get out of my damned tree. We don't want your sort around here.'

'Wow,' Pia said. 'Even the squirrels have a stuffy attitude in this part of town.'

The animal sat sulking at the end of the branch. It gnawed at something Pia hoped was a nut, rather than the last Brixtonian to enter the square.

She ignored her furry companion and zoomed into an expansive living room on the first floor. The white walls were splashed with colourful art and low modernist sofas reclined in the middle. The sole occupant was a short East Asian woman who wore an apron and polished a curved coffee table. The two floors above, generous bedrooms and en suite bathrooms, showed no further activity.

Pia sat back and let the camera hang around her neck. 'He's not home yet'. She sighed and shrugged at the squirrel who emitted a dismissive squeak and turned his back on her.

She sniggered and then glanced down, distracted by her phone vibrating in her jeans pocket. The screen flashed 'Mama' and her home phone number.

'Hola Mama.' Pia sighed with amusement. Her mother always had a sense of when Pia was up to something.

'Mija.' Her mother drew out the endearment. She'd lost none of her Spanish accent in the twenty-five years she'd spent in England, and Pia was always fond of that.

'Is it urgent Mama? I'm…' She peered around the square and garden beneath her feet. 'I'm quite busy.'

'What are you up to chica?' Her mother sounded suspicious.

'I'm working, Mama.'

Pia could hear her mother tut. 'It's only work if you get paid.'

'If I do this right I will get paid. I'm hoping quite a lot too.' She was irritated and hoped her target would appear so that she had an excuse to end the recurring argument with her mother.

'Make sure you do,' her mama snapped. 'Bueno. Will you be home for your dinner?'

'I said I would Mama.' Pia frowned wondering what her mother really wanted. 'Is that the only reason you're phoning?'

'Well…I was shopping in the market today…' Pia rolled her eyes. Here it comes. 'I was buying some beautiful peppers from the stall and that young woman, how do you call her?'

'Charlie.'

'Charlie. She's still single you know, and she's not busy tonight. I thought you could invite her round. I'll cook your favourite paella, open some red wine, and leave you two to—'

'Mama.' Pia cut her off.

'Mija. What is wrong with her? She is friendly. She has an honest job.'

'She gives you cheap veg.'

'You shouldn't joke. She is generous with food. A good thing in a woman. She would feed you up.'

4

'Mama. She's very nice.'

'Pretty too.'

'Yes, and she's pretty. But she just doesn't...' Pia stared into the middle distance thinking how to explain to her mother. Through the leaves she spotted the beautiful stranger again. The woman talked on her phone and wandered back towards the square. She held sun-streaked hair from her face, her arm soft and toned. Pia found herself admiring the attractive figure again: the sun-kissed skin, the generous breasts, the way she moved, elegant and at ease. That warm feeling tickled inside again and Pia sighed. 'She just doesn't have that magic. That something. I don't know.'

'Pia. You are waiting for a dream.' Pia tutted and slumped, digging in for the familiar admonishment. 'You want to be swept off your feet by a princess, but there are no princesses, and one day you'll wake up and you'll be an old woman and alone. You need someone to take care of you. To cook for you. To hold you tight at night.'

'Mama, how can you say that when you have Dad?'

'That's different. Things were different for us. And look where he is now. What use is a shining knight in armour when—'

Pia didn't hear her mother finish. A black Mercedes drew up in the space beneath her feet. The driver, dressed in a dark grey suit, marched around the car to open the back door. Out stepped Her Majesty's Member of Parliament for West Surrey. His full head of distinguished grey hair, which so captivated his female constituents, was in full view below.

'Mama,' Pia whispered. 'I have to go. I'll be home for dinner.'

The government minister moved away from the car and ignored the driver. The front door of the house was opened by a person unseen and a person disregarded. The minister disappeared inside and the driver returned to the car, unsurprised by the lack of acknowledgment, and left the square.

Pia's insides curdled at the thought of the politician, the most hard-lined immigration minister for decades, who rejected asylum requests from the most desperate of individuals. He lived a cozy life being served by the very people he wanted to expel from the country.

Pia zoomed in to the first floor where the maid was cleaning. She panned out to view the full width of the room and saw the minister step through the doorway. As soon as he entered, his face became stiff with irritation. The small woman bowed in apology and tried to leave the room clutching her duster and polish into her stomach. The minister sneered, his mouth ugly around a tirade of words inaudible to Pia but their intent clear.

But what Pia could hear was insistent chattering. She tried to ignore it. She clicked some images of the confrontation and concentrated on the scene at the end of the lens. But it blurred and appeared to become hairy.

'What the...?'

Pia took the camera away to find the proprietorial squirrel blocking her view.

'Oh no, not now. Shoo. Go away.'

Pia stretched higher, trying to shoot over the irritable animal. Inside the house, the minister shouted and gesticulated at the maid who raised her arms to protect herself. Pia squeezed on the shutter hoping to capture an incriminating moment.

Over the desperate snapping of the camera, the squirrel's squeals became louder and more insistent. Pia edged the camera away. She tried to keep shooting but was too unnerved by the animal's perseverance not to peek.

The small beast sat rigid on the branch. If a squirrel could growl and taunt it surely would be now. The wretched animal crouched down, wiggled its bottom and leapt forward.

'Shit!'

Its claws scratched on the bark as it tore towards her. As Pia jumped, she saw the minister raise his arm to strike. She squeezed her finger on the shutter and aimed in the direction of the house. She heard her camera rattle off photo after photo and focussed all her energy on pressing that button. At the same time she was aware of being surrounded by little other than air.

She felt light for a moment. Her stomach broke into butterflies. The ethereal sensation of spinning out of the tree was almost pleasant until she was brought back to almost earth.

Her belt snagged on a branch and snapped around her stomach. Her full weight plunged around the loop and it ripped the air out of her lungs. She hung upside down, winded, with her feet tangled and rattling in the twigs above.

Despite hanging in mid-air, she felt claustrophobic. As she breathed in her short painful breaths, soft fabric sucked and sealed around her mouth and nostrils. She opened her eyes to find the world glowed white with her T-shirt surrounding her face. She also registered a light breeze on her naked belly and partially naked breasts.

'Christ, are you all right?'

Although winded and feeling as if she were about to puke upside down into her own eyes, her tummy fluttered and heart beat a little faster. It was the unmistakable sound of the beautiful woman's voice.

2

Cate ambled along the route from the Tube station to Kensington Square for the last time. She gazed at the tall ornate buildings of Kensington High Street. She admired the formidable grey block of the art deco department store and took in the red flashes of double-decker buses that rumbled by. As she turned from the busy high street into the cool serenity of the garden square, she let its peace wash over her.

She sighed. She had loved living here. On the other side of the square she had a small studio flat above the art gallery. It had always been beyond her salary, but she had spent the most pleasant hours watching over the private gardens. She knew every tree and, through the leaves, every resident beyond the windows of the Georgian terraces.

A tight grip of panic and longing squeezed her chest. It grabbed her every time she realised what she was giving up. She tried to breathe it away in deep long exhalations. She was going to miss it. She took one last glance around the square, to bid farewell to her neighbours.

And it was only because of this procrastination that she spotted a shifty-looking young woman with short dark hair. She was attempting to appear nonchalant on the opposite side of the garden. What was she doing? The petite Mediterranean woman checked up and down the road and then hopped over the railings in an agile bound. Cate was too far away to hear what the woman said, but she appeared to be cursing. She lifted away a fragment of material from a railing and twirled around, chasing and patting her bum. Cate smiled when the woman removed her hand to reveal a pale patch of bottom shining through.

Cate's lift in mood was interrupted by her mobile.

'Hi Libby. I was about to call you.' At the same time she peeked through the trees and bushes to watch the cursing woman beyond.

'Sorry, what was that?' Cate said. 'Give me an hour sweetie.' She turned and sauntered back along the side road, attempting to hide her observation of the young woman. She peeked over her shoulder in time to see a pair of slim legs disappear into a tree.

The woman flailed around in the branches for a moment, spitting out a mouthful of leaves, and brought a camera with a large sports lens to her face.

'What the hell?' Cate said. 'No, sorry, not you darling.' The tinny sound of her best friend resumed from her phone and Cate crept back towards the gardens.

What was the petite woman up to? One of the cabinet ministers lived in that building. Was the woman paparazzi? Cate opened her mouth to shout, but the woman in the tree started waving her arms. Cate still couldn't hear. She could see her mouth moving, but who was she talking to?

A squirrel? She was talking to a squirrel. What on earth?

'Are you listening, Cate?' sounded louder in her ear.

'Sorry, what did you say? No really, I can't make sooner.' Cate allowed her friend to issue a tirade of warnings, all the while spying on the photographer. The squirrel had moved away. But the woman was still talking, gesturing with one arm with even more emphasis, and holding a phone with the other.

Cate wandered closer to the railings and began to pick out the odd word from the rapid fire in the tree above. Spanish. She was definitely speaking Spanish, but too quickly for Cate to understand.

This Spanish- and squirrel-speaking woman was quite the oddest member of the press that she'd encountered. Not wishing to be caught, Cate turned back up the street. A few moments later she recognised her neighbour's chauffeur turning into the square.

'This should be interesting... No, not you,' Cate said, as her friend squawked in her ear. 'I mean not that you're not interesting. Yes. I am listening. I will be there. I'll see you later,' and she tapped the phone dead.

Cate stood back and watched the scene unfold. The minister, one of the most unpleasant as far as she was concerned, entered the house and his car was driven away. Cate opened the gate with her resident's key and entered the garden. The young woman, unaware of Cate's presence, continued to take multiple pictures of the minister's house, and Cate tread closer.

In a blurred second, the woman cursed, a squirrel shrieked and branches and twigs cracked with the falling weight of photographer.

'Oh my God!' Cate leapt forward without thinking. If she had thought, attempting to break the woman's fall would have been a ludicrous thing to do, but her outstretched arms encountered only a falling camera.

The woman swung above her head, hooked over a branch. Her arms hung down towards the ground and her white T-shirt covered her face.

'Christ, are you all right?' Cate said.

The muffled reply from behind the T-shirt sounded strained. 'I feel a bit sick.'

'But are you hurt?'

'I feel a bit sick,' came the pathetic voice.

Cate grinned. The young woman hadn't come to much harm. Cate peered up at the petite figure that swayed upside down. She had slim legs, hugged tight by her black jeans. Her toned stomach was exposed and Cate noticed her inviting and flawless skin. She peeped down at the bra, which glowed white against a dark Mediterranean complexion, and allowed herself to notice what a very poor job it was doing of supporting the ample breasts now it was the wrong way up.

Cate gathered herself and put down the camera.

'Here. Let's cover you up.' She lifted the young woman's T-shirt and tucked it beneath her belt. The sight of the revealed bright red face made her laugh. 'We need to get you down before you explode.'

She put her hands beneath the woman's arms and supported her head on her shoulder while the woman wriggled free. With a crack from a branch and a thud on the ground the curious photographer landed back on earth. She groaned and held her stomach. When the blood had receded from the photographer's cheeks, Cate was taken aback by what a pretty face she had. She was fine-featured with beautiful lips. Large brown irises and inky eyelashes made her appear like a small helpless animal rather than a beast of the paparazzi. She was a few years younger than Cate, early twenties she guessed.

'You caught my camera,' the young woman said. Her voice was strained with discomfort but she sounded surprised. She stretched out across the grass.

'Oh no you don't.' Cate snatched up the camera and the photographer was still too winded to complain. 'I'm not mean enough to leave you hanging in a tree, but I can't let you take candid shots of my neighbours. Let's see what you were up to.'

Cate flicked back through the pictures on the camera screen. The first were blurred photos of leaves and branches and a little bit of squirrel. A few had caught the minister's house but were too indistinct to be intrusive.

But the next captured the maid covering her head and ducking out of the room. She was wincing and cowering. Cate flicked back to reveal a sequence in reverse that looked like the minister drawing his hand away from the employee. Then Cate halted at a clear photo. The minister's hand was thrust back and his face had such cruel intent that it was impossible to misinterpret the scene.

Cate regarded the young woman. 'Do you know what you have here?'

'Did I get it?' She looked both worried and excited. When Cate turned the camera screen to her, joy lit up her face.

'Got the bastard,' she said.

Cate considered her. 'What is your intention with these?'

'Sell them to every single newspaper. I want everyone to know what a hypocritical shit that so-called respectable minister is.'

'Really?' Cate said, wondering at such a vehement response. 'So what is your argument with him?'

The young woman's expression soured into one of distaste. 'He turns down every single asylum request from gay people. He wants to cap immigration numbers to countries he knows are tyrannical and all in the name of maintaining British values. I want people to know what his values really are.'

Cate flicked her gaze between the passionate woman sitting on the ground and the camera screen as she clicked back through the grainy images. She saw the angry exchange from end to beginning with the minister stepping through the door. Then the shots switched to a bright sharp picture of children.

Cate stepped back with the change of scene. The background was cloudy skies and grey concrete high-rise flats. Three small children stood on a pile of rubble dressed in old clothes, drained of colour from countless washes. But their expressions sparkled. Cate wondered what the photographer must have said to make their faces beam with such glee. Their rosy cheeks were a splash of colour in the barren setting, which resonated with flashes of red poppies growing in the rubble beyond.

Cate peeked at the earnest young woman on the grass, her face still vivid with passion and determination.

'What's your name?' Cate asked gently.

'Pia. Pia Benitez-Smith.'

Cate smiled. 'Well, Pia Benitez-Smith. I think you're a very talented photographer, and one whose heart is in the right place.'

Cate was about to hand over the camera, but noticed that Pia's demeanor had changed. She appeared vulnerable all of a sudden. Her eyes were wide and her features soft with awe. The change from the ferocious photographer spitting out words against the minister was perplexing. Cate knelt down. Pia's shocked stare followed her.

'Are you all right?' Cate said, reaching out to hold her face.

She touched her cheek with the very tip of her fingers. The sensation of Pia's soft warm skin thrilled her senses. Her fingertips tingled. The pleasure hummed through her arms and fluttered deep inside. She couldn't move. She was like a statue, albeit one whose heart beat quick and whose blood ran hot.

'I'm fine thank you,' Pia said, blinking over those huge eyes. Deepest, hazel eyes, with blackest pupils engulfing them. Cate found herself being drawn closer, enthralled by the dark pools, wanting to peer deeper and deeper. For a moment their gazes locked and the young woman stared back with the same intense consumption. It felt like Pia could see right through her: every atom, every secret, every moment of Cate's life.

'I'm fine,' Pia whispered.

Cate twitched back. 'Good,' she said flushing. The moment was broken. She laughed away her embarrassment at their intimacy and withdrew her hand. 'Yes, good.' And she thrust the camera towards Pia.

Cate brushed away blades of grass from her knees and stood up. 'Now. You'd better hurry and send off those pictures, if you want to catch the dailies.'

Pia still stared at her with a wide open mouth.

Cate coughed to clear her throat. 'And much as though I applaud your exposure of the right honorable minister, and hope very much that his wife kicks him out and takes care of the servants, please do not let me catch you here again.' She tried to sound serious but her mouth wouldn't stop lifting in amusement.

'Good luck Pia Benitez-Smith.' Cate turned and left the garden, and all the while she felt the young woman's eyes on her back.

3

It had all happened so quickly that Pia stared in shock after the beautiful woman. She'd had trouble enough paying intelligent attention while her tummy recovered from its painful throttling. She'd put what little energy she had left into not checking the woman up and down. But when she'd said her name in those velvet tones, complimented her work and started to reach out to touch her, Pia's mind had blanked into submission.

The woman had mesmerised her. At that moment she could have commanded Pia to rob a bank and she would have complied. As it was she stared, oblivious to time and place, everything a blur, all except the woman with the sun shining through her hair and the voice that could stun a rampaging elephant into submission.

And it was with the same brainless expression that Pia watched her walk away. The woman's hips swayed as she wandered through the green shade of the garden. She became smaller and smaller, left the confines of the railings and disappeared into a doorway on the corner of the square. Pia didn't know how long she stared, but it dawned on her that she'd effectively followed the woman home. She snapped her head around, not wanting to stalk.

What was her name? She hadn't even asked her name.

Pia checked the camera for the last photograph the woman had seen. It was the one she'd taken of children as she walked past the tower blocks that morning. She'd heard their giggling as they rambled about on an old pile of chippings and concrete blocks. A few metres away, their mother grappled with a small baby in a pram that wanted its feet rather than its bottom in a nappy.

'Excuse me. Could I take a photo of your kids?' Pia had asked.

'What for?' the woman said over her shoulder.

'I'm trying to get a photograph for an exhibition. It's called Beauty in Unexpected Places. Your kids look so happy playing on the rubble. I thought they were beautiful.'

'Ha! Those little buggers? Yeah, knock yourself out love.' And the woman had returned her attention to the baby who'd pulled the nappy over its face.

Pia'd had one chance to take a photograph before the children noticed her. They'd glanced up, their engrossed and genuine smiles still lingering on their faces, and she'd snapped the scene. It had captured their essence and she didn't need to take any more.

Pia felt pride warm her belly as she thought of the beautiful woman admiring her work and, without thinking, gazed towards the building she'd entered.

'Wow,' Pia whispered, numbed by the whole encounter.

The sensation of the cold hard camera in her hands worked its way into her consciousness.

'Shit, I need to send these off.'

She flicked forward through the pictures, watching the scene that she'd missed. The photo the woman had shown had been the best one. She had a good eye. With a rising sense of excitement Pia transferred the image to her phone. There was no time for cropping or adjusting the image back home. She fumbled an email to her agent and selected send with trembling fingers.

Pia got to her feet and breathed out. She paced under the trees, not knowing what to do. She rubbed her hands together hoping the agent would find a buyer or two, happy to expose the minister. At least a minute passed and Pia began to get twitchy and wondered if she should call. She held the phone in her hands, squeezing it and drumming her fingers on the screen.

A jolt of excitement sparked though her when the phone vibrated.

'Hi. Did you get it?' Pia babbled into the phone.

'Pia, this is gold,' her old agent rasped. 'It's a bit late in the day, but do you want to hold out for an exclusive buyer on this?'

Pia paced the garden in short agitated steps. 'No. Get it into as many papers, news channels, anywhere that you can.'

'Are you sure? You could get a few thousand for this if you played it right.'

'I just want it out there.'

Her agent remained quiet on the other end of the phone.

'Please,' Pia said.

'You know,' her agent started, 'you and your mum would find several thousand very helpful.'

Pia hesitated for a fraction of a second at the thought of her mother. 'Perhaps. But it might not sell at all if we play it badly. I want it out now.'

'All right. All right. I'm on it.' And her agent rang off.

Pia slumped onto a bench and held her phone. She willed her agent to call back, despite a matter of seconds passing.

A text message buzzed. 'Give me time. Have a drink or something. I know you're waiting by your phone.'

Pia chuckled at the message. Her agent knew her too well. A little more relaxed, she turned her attention to her camera. She flicked forward through the scene and analysed each photo for any redeemable qualities. Test shot. Blurred. Inferior version of the sent photo. Nice picture of a tree and sky, and a portrait of a squirrel peering down from the safety of a familiar branch.

Pia coughed out a wry laugh. 'You little...'

'You're still here.'

The honeyed voice was unmistakeable and Pia jumped up.

'Hi,' Pia said. 'I'm sorry. I'm so glad to see you again. I didn't ask your name or thank you.'

It was fortunate that she hadn't had time to think before speaking, because when she focussed on the woman all coherent thought left her.

The woman smiled. 'Catherine. Or Cate. Please call me Cate.'

Pia vaguely registered the name. But she was far more attentive to her dress and what it covered, or didn't, at least not very well. She wore a white silk dress held up by a single wide strap around the shoulder that left her upper chest bare even of jewellery. The soft material cradled her breasts and Pia didn't need a second glance to know that Cate didn't wear a bra. It was more revealing in a way, more suggestive, than being naked, and as Pia surveyed the thin material she was left in no doubt as to the shapeliness of Cate's legs.

Pia heard a cough and found Cate staring at her, as if expecting a response.

'Muh?' Pia said.

Cate frowned. 'Are you sure you're all right?'

'Mmmm.'

Pia blushed as Cate bent down and stared at her. She watched Cate's eyes flick between hers and her forehead crease in concern. Her irises shimmered between grey and blue and Pia's lips opened in awe.

'Are you sure you didn't bump your head when you fell?' Cate asked.

Pia watched the creases on Cate's forehead deepen and admired the shape of her eyebrows: two perfect arches that curved in the middle in a question. Pia opened her mouth, but the facility of speech was still absent. She shook her head, slowly and deliberately.

'Do you live nearby? Can I take you home?' Cate said, her eyebrows now crinkling with puzzlement.

Pia shook her head, a dozy smile on her face.

Cate glanced at the thin golden watch on her bare arm and frowned at Pia. 'I think I should take you to sit down somewhere. I need to check that you're all right.'

Without fully registering why Cate was concerned, Pia let her arm slide into hers and was led away in a pleasant haze.

—

Pia followed Cate into the Roof Garden Restaurant high above the old Kensington department store. Cate stood with serene poise, holding her black clutch bag, as they waited to be seated.

Pia wondered if she looked as shifty and scruffy as she suspected, and she fidgeted with the strap on her rucksack. She felt as if she'd been pulled backwards through a hedge, except it had been a tree. She stood out, incongruous in the crisp white restaurant with its floral wallpaper accents and modern bar. Even the linen tablecloths were without blemish. At least the restaurant was quiet with only one or two tables of well-dressed early evening diners.

Cate turned back to her. 'Are you OK? They shouldn't be too long.'

'I'm fine,' Pia said, trying to sound at ease. 'I've never thought of coming up here. Too posh for me.'

Cate's lips curled in amusement. 'You are showing quite a bit of cheek coming in here tonight.'

'Really?' And then Pia realised what Cate had meant as she registered the feeling of exposure on her left buttock. She whipped her hand around to cover her bottom.

Cate laughed. 'It's fine. Your T-shirt almost hides it. Almost.'

A young man dressed in black from head to toe recognised Cate and escorted them to a table by the long window spanning the length of the room. Pia half heard Cate order a glass of sparkling water for Pia and a coffee for herself.

'Take a seat madam. It won't be a moment,' the waiter said, but Pia was too choked by the view to respond. She was a life-long admirer of London and the panorama took her breath away. She could see over the pointed and curling red-grey rooftops of the great houses of Kensington, to the dome of the Albert Hall. The luscious green trees of the parks broke through the skyline and in the distance the Gherkin and London Eye peeked back at her.

She caught Cate smiling. 'It's good isn't it?'

'Amazing.' Pia wished she could snap away with her camera.

'Sit down and have a drink.' Cate pointed to the glass the unobtrusive waiter had left. 'I want you to rest and check that you're all right.'

No sooner had Pia planted her bottom in the chair, her phone buzzed. She snatched it up.

'It's my agent,' she said, grinning at Cate. 'The photo's been picked up by *The Guardian*.'

'I bet it has. Congratulations. That's quite a scoop.'

Pia shuffled around in her chair, full of excitement. Another text vibrated her phone.

'Oh, the Beeb are going to use it too.' Pia couldn't contain her elation, but sat still when she noticed Cate appeared serious.

'You didn't go for an exclusive?'

Pia shook her head 'No. I want that photo to be printed everywhere.'

Cate nodded. 'Yes of course you do.' She leaned forward in amused conspiracy. 'Are you really paparazzi? You don't strike me as the usual type.'

'Actually I'm a bit crap at it,' admitted Pia. 'It's not what I do full-time. Well not the exposé type of work.'

Cate raised an eyebrow. 'So what do you do when you're not hanging around Kensington Square?'

Pia smiled. 'Freelance photography at the moment. I've been taking pictures at local events and flogging them to any rag that'll have them. Sometimes I get lucky and see a celeb out and about, but taking pictures of people skulking around in sunglasses isn't my favourite job.'

'What is then?'

Pia leaned forward so that she was only a foot away from Cate. 'I love taking candid photos, capturing people's natural expressions,' She looked away to think of a way to explain what thrilled her about it. 'When it's an unguarded instant of joy or when something moves them you see who they really are for a moment.' She turned back to Cate and could see she had her full attention. Pia shrugged. 'But catching famous people messing up like the rest of us; that's not fun for me. I like to capture people's honest moments, but honestly.'

'But spying on someone like the immigration minister is fine?'

Pia sniggered. 'Yes. I don't mind uncovering someone being nasty, especially if they're being dishonest or hypocritical.'

Cate's expression flickered between approval and another emotion that she covered too quickly for Pia to discern. She blinked and her features relaxed into a soft amused expression. Her eyes never left Pia's and shifted between grey and green as a shadow stroked across her face.

'Do you think you are good at reading people?' Cate said.

'From their expressions? What they're thinking?' Pia asked.

Cate nodded.

'My dad says I am. He says I have an artist's eye. I'm always people-watching and wondering who they are, what they do for a living and what they're talking about. I get a lot of practice observing.' She shrugged. 'But then Mama says I see what I want to see.' And she giggled.

'And what do you see Pia Benitez-Smith?' Cate sat up in her chair, inviting observation.

Pia hesitated, surprised by the raw question. She considered for a moment whether she should be polite, and then decided to answer with her customary honesty. 'I see a beautiful woman who is considered and intelligent, and kind to strangers who fall out of trees.'

She'd hoped to amuse Cate, but her expression remained unmoved, her mouth parting as if about to respond. Their eyes remained locked and Pia's insides chilled with the fear that she'd been impertinent.

Cate's mobile buzzed on the table. She scrabbled for it and tapped it silent. A flicker of regret disturbed her features and Pia wondered where Cate should be in her elegant evening dress.

Pia expected her to make excuses but her hesitancy hung heavy around them. Pia thought she should make it easy and stood up. 'I'm feeling fine now. I can make my way home. Please don't hang around for my sake.'

Cate looked up, her expression still serious. 'Would you stay? Have one more drink with me?'

4

'This is bonkers.' Pia leaned on the white railing of the art deco terrace, a second cool glass of Champagne in her hand. Below, spread across the roof of the old department store, was an English woodland garden, lush and incongruous. It glowed warm in the low evening sun.

'I knew there were gardens up here, but I didn't expect trees.'

Cate smiled and pointed across the lawns and treetops to a pool. 'They have one or two flamingos in the pond.'

'Mad,' Pia said grinning. 'Wonderful and barking mad.'

Pia scanned around, trying to find her bearings. 'The square's that way isn't it? You're just a stone's throw away.' She was conscious of being a virtual stranger but knowing Cate's address. She added. 'I live over in Brixton. Great place to live but there's nothing quite like this.'

'But there's a price to pay for the privilege of living here,' Cate said, still staring over the gardens.

'It's expensive enough in Brixton.' Pia tutted. 'I still live with my mum. I don't think either of us could afford to do anything else.'

Cate looked surprised. 'Do you get on? Is it all right living at home?'

'Oh Mama's great. I'm very lucky. She's like a best friend to me, and she's always been supportive of who I am. I've some gay friends whose parents have been terrible. Oh. I'm gay by the way,' Pia said, struck by the way she talked to Cate as if she'd known her far longer than the hour they'd shared.

Cate smiled indulgently. 'I know. It's written all over you.'

'Is it? Oh.' Pia shook her head. 'I have no gaydar at all, so I assume people don't spot me. I'm always surprised by the people who leap out of the closet. I pride myself on capturing people's intimate moments on camera and spotting the emotions they hide, but I'm buggered if I can tell they're gay.'

Cate raised an amused eyebrow.

Pia opened her mouth to speak, but stopped. She'd been on the verge of asking about Cate's sexuality. But it seemed rude about someone who was clearly more private than Pia. She also didn't want to appear presumptuous, as if Cate's sexuality had a bearing on their interaction.

'Yes Mama's brilliant,' Pia said, instead returning to safe ground. 'Although she is always telling me to get a proper job.' She pursed her lips and squinted at Cate. 'Maybe she does want me to move my sorry arse out after all.'

Cate laughed and Pia beamed, lifted by the euphoria of causing Cate's happiness.

'I think it's natural for a mother to worry about her daughter,' Cate said, her joy still brightening her face.

'She wants me to get a normal job though, something boring and predictable. She thinks photojournalism doesn't pay enough and it's too risky.'

Cate's face creased deeper with amusement. 'Your run in with a squirrel and near miss with the ground might prove her point. And a member of the paparazzi with scruples might not be the highest earner, no matter how talented and enchanting.'

Pia's insides fluttered, exhilarated by Cate's words, but were light with fear that she'd misheard. She blinked and tried to appear unmoved while her mind raced with the idea

26

that Cate found her enchanting. She floundered for a moment and gulped her Champagne, before attempting to gloss over the pause.

'Yeah. I understand why Mama worries. About me in particular.' She calmed her nerves and turned to Cate. 'You know the phrase "thick as thieves". Well that's my dad and brother. Both as bloody stupid as each other.'

Cate frowned in a question.

'They are both currently detained at Her Majesty's pleasure.' Pia tutted. 'Silly buggers.'

'They're in prison?'

'Yeah. They got caught up in an illegal financial scheme, the gullible pair. The guy who conned them got away scot free.'

'Is that what your dad does for a living. Finance?' Cate was surprised.

'No.' Pia shook her head. 'That's not him at all. Which was part of the problem. He used to be in the army. He met Mama when he was stationed in Gibraltar.' Pia grinned at Cate. She itched with excitement, wanting to tell her favourite story. 'They fell in love with a single look across a café.'

'Oh really.' Cate sounded amused and disbelieving.

'Really.' Pia nodded. 'It was where Mama worked, a small café in the hills. Dad always told me he'd been out walking and stopped for water. But their eyes met when he walked through the door. He stayed all afternoon and spent his week's money hoping she would talk to him.'

'And did she fall for him as quickly?'

'Oh yes. Much to the consternation of Mama's family.' Pia laughed. 'My grandparents tried to keep them apart; sent Mama to live with an aunt in Andalucia. I think they wanted her to marry one of her cousins. A respectable well-paid lawyer in Madrid. But Dad couldn't forget her. He spent months trying to find her between tours and, when he did, he whisked her back to England and never let her go.'

27

'They eloped?' Cate said, her lips lingering open in surprise.

'Yes.' Pia beamed.

'That is very romantic.' Cate's cheer faded. 'And now? All these years later?'

'It's still a true romance. But it has been difficult.' Pia shuffled, a little uncomfortable. 'Dad had trouble finding work when he left the forces. Couldn't settle into anything. He's a very gifted artist in fact. It's a shame he couldn't find anything creative.'

'That must be where you get your good eye from.'

Pia blushed at the compliment. 'I hope so. But he's very good. I try to capture people's genuine personalities on camera, but he gets them better with a brushstroke.' She ran her fingers through her short hair, fidgeting at an uncomfortable memory. 'I was in my parents' bedroom once, when I was about twelve,' she said, feeling shy. 'I found one of his paintings of Mama at the back of their wardrobe. She was posed in bed with rosy cheeks and the sheets pulled up over her chest. He'd caught such an intense look of love and lust on her face. It was shocking. I still find it a bit embarrassing to think of it.'

'They sound like they adore each other.' Cate's plain tone verged on regret.

'They do. I love that they didn't let anything get in their way. Just how it should be for a true love.'

Cate gave her a sad smile. 'I can see even more why your mum would like you to have a secure job though.'

Pia sighed, thinking she knew what Cate meant. 'Yes, I know. But Dad says I should try to make a career out of photography first, even if I have to scrape by on the wage. He says that you have to follow your heart, otherwise hearts have a habit of breaking.'

Pia didn't know if Cate had heard her. She gazed over the rooftops towards Hyde Park and Pia sensed that she needed a moment to herself. Pia sipped at her Champagne, which had lubricated her tongue, and fidgeted with all the patience of a hungry dog shown its dinner.

'What about you?' Pia said, after all of thirty seconds.

Cate turned back looking amused. 'What about me?'

'Love or money?'

Cate's eyes flicked between the distance and Pia. Her cheeks coloured. 'I don't think it's as simple as that.'

Pia remained quiet but waited, anticipating Cate's elaboration.

'My mother wasn't well off,' Cate said. 'She had expensive taste, which made her very unhappy, and I think I take after her.'

'Do you?' Pia failed to keep quiet. 'I had you down as a posh girl. You speak proper and all,' she said, putting on a strong East End accent. 'And you live in Kensington.'

'I was lucky. I went to a good school. I had a scholarship. And again, of sorts, to go to Cambridge.'

'Wow. What did you study? Politics? Law? Something high-powered like that?'

Cate's face lightened. 'English.'

Pia chuckled. 'That's what all the mercenary types choose.'

'Yes, perhaps I should have chosen law,' Cate admitted, staring past Pia as she thought. 'But reading great literature on the college lawns of the Cambridge Backs, that's one of life's rare privileges.' She switched her focus back to Pia, the love from remembering those days still soft in her expression.

Pia tilted her head. 'See. You are a romantic.'

Cate laughed and turned to her with that wonderful smile. Her eyes glistened and her face shone with unguarded joy. Cate reached out to squeeze Pia's arm with those long, elegant fingers and Pia's gaze followed the pleasing curve of her naked arm all the way to her shoulders, slim neck and exquisite face. Its beauty made her ache inside.

'I think you're an incurable romantic, Ms Benitez-Smith,' Cate said with unrestrained warmth.

Pia's skin thrilled at the encounter. Her body hummed with pleasure radiating out from where they touched. Her limbs felt weak and beyond her control. Without thinking she lifted her arm, its intent to wrap around Cate's slim waist and pull her close.

'Excuse me,' Cate said distracted. She searched her bag and took out a phone that buzzed.

Pia breathed out and tried to shake off her body's irresistible attraction to Cate, in case she should lose control and reach out again.

Cate didn't answer her phone. She stared at it, dejected, and stroked the screen to reject the call. She lifted her gaze to Pia, her face heavy with regret.

'I'm very late,' Cate said.

'Somewhere you don't want to be?'

'Actually a party. A hen party.'

'No wonder you don't want to go.' Pia giggled. She wondered at the event Cate must be missing for it to warrant the dress she wore with such elegance. Not a pub crawl with learner plates she imagined, but still not an evening she'd enjoy. 'I feel like such a tortured fish out of water at those things,' she added.

Cate smiled and looked at her, her eyes dark and betraying longing.

'One more drink?' Pia whispered. 'Please.'

———

They sat side by side on recliners, gazing out to the crimson sky, the deep red orb of the sun about to extinguish beneath the skyline. They lounged, relaxed after more Champagne, although Cate managed it with rather more elegance than Pia.

Pia didn't care. She was bathed in the setting sun and the gentle dim lights of the restaurant. The conversation from diners murmured and sparkled around them and the sound of London's Friday night traffic below seemed far away.

Buoyed by the alcohol, Pia stole a not too subtle glance at Cate in profile. She had an intelligent face, high forehead and perfect straight nose. Pia lingered on her full red lips, licking her own, and returned her attention to the long eyelashes that blinked lazy and relaxed.

Cate took a slow sip of Champagne and peeked at Pia, her lips twitching in the corners. 'I know you're watching me.'

'I can't tell the colour of your eyes,' Pia said.

'They change.' Cate turned towards Pia, tucking up her knees and resting her head on her arm. 'It depends on what I'm wearing and the light. If I wear blue, it tends to bring out a slate grey, if green then a pale green.'

Pia was unable to hide her admiration. 'They're amazing. Mine are boring. Just hazel.'

'Honest eyes,' Cate said with a serious tone, and then: 'But I wouldn't call deep hypnotic hazel boring. Not with those long inky eyelashes.'

The words made Pia warm inside. She peered across to the skyline. 'This is perfect. Champagne on a summer's evening, a beautiful view and beautiful company. What more could you ask for?'

A thrill of fear shot through her. She'd uttered the words without thinking, with that fluidity that Champagne brings.

Cate regarded her. 'You're easy to please.'

'It's that expensive taste again isn't it?' Pia said grinning.

'Perfect evenings do tend to be expensive. Champagne for instance.' Cate raised her glass and an eyebrow.

Pia giggled. 'True. Although it would be just as good with Prosecco.' She shrugged. 'But I don't think perfect evenings have to be expensive. Although, a night at the

Savoy wouldn't be too shabby. I've always had a daydream of staying at the Savoy. Champagne, a view of the river, lying in bed with a woman I adore in my arms.'

Cate's expression was unreadable. 'That's a lovely daydream and not all that expensive. I think you have a wonderful attitude.'

Pia swung her legs off the recliner and sat up. 'Come on. What's your idea of a perfect evening?'

Cate showed the pearls of her teeth in that perfect smile. She cast her gaze to the distance. 'Oh gosh, where to begin? A perfect night. I suppose there would have to be music. I don't think it matters what type. Something to move me. Whether to dance or to tears I don't think it matters, but an exceptional performance of its kind.'

Pia nodded, 'That doesn't sound too unreasonable.'

'Well, tickets to the Albert Hall to see top performers aren't going to be cheap. And, of course, I would have to have a first-class seat.'

'Jeeez,' Pia said, 'You'll be expecting dinner too.'

'Of course.'

'And I suppose that would have to be a Michelin-starred restaurant?'

'Not necessarily. They don't cover some types of food well, but I would expect it to be the pinnacle of whichever cuisine was chosen.'

Pia nodded again. 'Not unreasonable.'

'And then a surprise. A little bit of magic that I didn't expect to end the evening.'

'Like a walk under the stars or dancing in the moonlight?' Pia said, her excitement carrying her away.

'Yes. Perhaps a swim in tropical seas under the stars.'

'Oh,' Pia said.

'So you see.' Cate tilted her head to the side. 'Expensive.'

Pia considered Cate, and what she'd desired. She started to giggle. 'I think I could show you an evening like that, perhaps all within a mile of here.'

'Really? On a freelance photographer's wage?'

'I think I could,' Pia said, a broad grin on her face. 'For less than a hundred pounds, perhaps less than a tenner.'

Cate frowned at her, challenging her to explain.

But Pia's enthusiasm and bubbles of Champagne got the better of her. She put out her hand to Cate. 'Do you want to see?'

Cate stared at her, eyes wide. She glanced down to Pia's hand and Pia's stomach somersaulted as she watched her infectious enthusiasm lift Cate's face with the thrill of conspiracy.

Pia trembled with nerves. 'Come on.'

Cate stuck out her hand and Pia beamed. Dizzy with excitement, she led Cate from the exclusive Kensington rooftops to the London streets below and into the night.

5

They were buffeted by warm air as they stepped into the street, baked by the summer's day. Pia squinted along the orange-lit road, loomed over by ornate brick buildings chequered with lights. Shops closing, flats returning to life.

'Let's go along the High Street,' Pia said. She took Cate's hand, soft fingers between hers. 'Towards Hyde Park.'

Cate squeezed her hand and tugged her back. 'You're not going to tell me you have tickets for the Albert Hall?' She had a suspicious look on her face.

Pia grinned. 'No. Not up in the gods for you today. We're going underground.'

They ducked off the main road down narrower residential streets with Georgian terraces five stories high. They passed small cobbled passageways and streets of old servants houses, now the property of the wealthy. They dashed across the tree-lined arterial road and cut around the gardens of the Natural History Museum. Cate's heels chattered over the pavement as they hurried past the looming towers of the great gothic building.

'Down here,' Pia said, slowing as they turned the corner at the railings and descended the steps into the subway. They wandered along the wide brown tunnel that flickered in the harsh fluorescent lights. People flowed up and down and across in front of them: flagging tourists, city workers eager to get home and music lovers late for a concert at the Albert Hall.

Cate glanced at her, unsure, questioning why Pia had brought them here, but above the cacophony of short irritable exchanges, desperate pleas for directions and the footfall of hundreds, Pia heard familiar haunting notes.

She could see Cate wrinkle her eyebrows trying to peer ahead. She slowed and released Pia's hand as the music became more distinct. At first, with only the odd phrase reaching them, it sounded like a woman singing a beautiful and mournful Jewish prayer. As they got closer, the sound seamlessly blended into the music of a violin, the long held notes soaring like a soprano before the more heart-breaking sequences cried out in perfectly wrought string notes.

The effect was enchanting and Pia could feel them both being lured through the busy crowd. The music sounded close, and all of a sudden the stream of people parted to reveal an old man playing a violin with inhuman flair and understanding.

He wore jeans and an old checked shirt, which had seen better decades, and a silk scarf around his neck, the threads pulled by the old man's stubble which gleamed white against his black skin. His yellowing eyes were fixed in front of him, unblinking and unseeing.

The sight made the music all the more incredible to Pia, watching him draw the bow across the strings and hearing the grieving sound of Ravel's *Kaddish* sing out. It grabbed her heart and choked her throat with emotion.

Cate had stopped. She stared at the musician transfixed, her hand drawn to her chest. She didn't seem to notice people bustling by, irritable at her obstruction. Careful not to make a sound, Pia picked up a crate that lay next to the musician's violin case and drew Cate out of the flow of traffic. She sat beside her, and at no point did Cate's gaze waver from the violinist. She sat, hypnotised, her hands placed in prayer to her lips.

Pia sat glowing with pride at the old blind Trinidadian who had cast a spell. She looked around to see the effect on

36

others. At first, only small children were caught by the music. They stared at Cate and stopped before being tugged along by impatient parents. But one refused to move. A small boy stood his ground, and his tired mother resigned herself to listen. After a few bars her face softened and her grip relaxed on the child. She became entranced by the music.

The pace of passersby began to slow. More and more turned to watch as they made their way. A group of students stopped and listened, one open-mouthed, another recording on his phone. Soon a crowd had gathered and anyone wanting to carry on their journey had to squeeze along the walls.

At its finale the music became quieter, and softer. Its solemn final note held the audience before it disappeared echoing down the tunnel.

Cate leapt up and applauded, her ecstatic smile squeezing a tear from her eye. The crowd followed with glee and the sound of applause was accompanied by the chink of coins thrown into the old musician's case.

The crowd dispersed and only the elated Pia and Cate remained when the musician put down his violin and bow. He tapped his foot towards the space left by the crate and then he stared up, his unfocussed eyes aimed straight at Pia.

'Pia Benitez-Smith,' he said in a rich Caribbean accent. 'I hope that's you who's nicked my crate.'

'How the hell did you know it was me?'

His laughter was deep and cracked with the years. 'Who else comes and listens to old Spencer?'

'More people should,' Cate said. 'That was incredible.'

Spencer's head twitched in Cate's direction. 'Well hello. Who have you brought, Pia?'

Pia stepped beside Cate, proud of her new friend's appreciation of her old. 'This is Cate.' She beamed up in admiration. 'I wanted to show her that you don't need to spend the earth to hear music that can move it.'

Spencer chuckled. He put out his hand, his thick grey fingers reaching towards Cate. With a natural movement she placed her hand in his and Spencer leaned down to kiss her fingers. 'Always a pleasure to meet a beautiful woman.'

Pia rolled her eyes at the old man's charm. 'Oh come on Spencer. I'd never deny she's beautiful, but you can't tell that from her voice.'

'No, that's true.' Spencer chuckled. 'But I can from yours. I can tell a smitten woman when I hear one.'

Pia blushed so deep it burned all the way to her ears. She could see Cate was amused, but she tactfully kept turned away.

Spencer crouched down to sort the money. 'I think I can call it a night by the sound of that collection.'

'Oh let me,' Cate said. She bent down to fetch the silver and gold coins that had bounced out of the case. Her dress opened at the back and flowed around her body as she leant down. Pia warmed inside at the sight of Cate helping her friend.

—

They ambled into the darkness of Hyde Park, the humid air close around them. Cate swung her high heels by her side and walked barefoot through the grass. As they walked further from the luminous orange of the main road, Pia's sight grew accustomed to the ambient light and she began to recognise the shape of trees and infrequent passersby. Pia could make out Cate's content face, still on a high after being purged by an emotional piece.

'How do you know Spencer?' Cate's voice was relaxed and soft in the steamy air.

'I've known him most of my life.' Pia replied. 'He lives next door. We're in an old terrace and he has a garden flat next door to us.'

'Why doesn't he play professionally? He's extraordinary.'

'He did. I think.' Pia tried to recall. 'I'm pretty sure he played as part of the Philharmonic when I was little. Mama said he froze one day, in a concert, couldn't remember the notes, and he couldn't check the sheet music like the others. I think he just lost his confidence.'

'But couldn't he do other work? Recordings?'

'He says he's happy busking.' Pia shrugged.

'But that must pay almost nothing.'

Pia laughed. 'He's happy with what he's got. Is that so hard to believe?'

'Even those happy with the simplest things still need something to live on.'

'He says he has enough to eat. His family, a son and grandchildren, live in London. He has friends from over forty years in Brixton.' Pia smiled. 'I think he has a very nice life.'

Cate hesitated for a moment. 'Things money can't buy,' she said under her breath.

'I think he's very lucky,' Pia added. 'And I think he appreciates it too.'

'Is he a role model for you?' Cate asked, her light mischievousness returned.

They'd reached the bank of the Serpentine. Pia stared across the lake's dark expanse, watching the reflection of the half moon quivering on the still waters.

'I admire him very much. I adore his playing and it's difficult not to love someone who is so content and full of life.'

Cate's face was a blur in the dim light. Pia only caught her smile and her nod out of the corner of her eye. Cate sighed and put her hands on her hips and gazed up towards the sky.

'You can see stars.' She stepped back, surprised. The brightest stars shone through the faint city glow. 'You know, I'd given up on the night sky in London. I had no idea you could see them.'

'You can't beat seeing the stars.' Pia grinned, and added: 'Or swimming beneath them.'

It was quiet for a moment before she heard Cate's laugh rise. 'You can't go swimming in the Serpentine.'

'Yes you can.' Pia enjoyed catching out her companion. 'The Lido's just there if you're not brave enough to swim in the open water.'

'Do they have costumes for hire?'

'Oh, it's shut now. But last time I tried I didn't find my costume essential for swimming.'

'You're serious?'

Pia had already taken Cate's hand and was leading her towards the Lido building. The tables and chairs on the bank outside were deserted and a cool white beam shone from the empty kitchen through the columns of the classic building. Here, Cate's face was a little more clear, as was her look of amused affront.

'Pia Benitez-Smith. Are you trying to get me out of my clothes?'

'I'm just granting you your wish,' Pia said, delighting in the fulfilment, and the added bonus of perhaps seeing Cate undress.

'Well, if you promise not to look.'

'I can't promise that.' Pia giggled. 'But if you don't have the guts to swim in the...'

She'd expected Cate to stall and take her time to tip-toe into the lake. But with a smooth movement Cate had slipped from her dress, stepped out of her underwear and was gracefully dipping into the water.

Pia stared, the sight of Cate's naked body, her toned back, the curve of her hips, the long slim legs, having the same effect as a temporary lobotomy. She gawped as Cate glided out in a breast stroke, disappearing into the darkness without a sound.

'Pia!' Cate called. 'Close your mouth and come in. It's wonderful.'

Pia twitched back into consciousness. 'Um. OK. Yes. Err. Will do.'

She checked around the dark edge of the park and hid her rucksack under a table. She slipped off her Converse trainers and hopped about on the bank peeling off her tight jeans. She flung her T-shirt over a metal chair and dipped her toe in the water.

It was warm and tickled where the water slipped over her foot and stroked around her leg. She slid into the depths and pushed out towards Cate. The water caressed her breasts and licked between her legs as she moved. It was such a sensual experience. She felt more naked in the water as it flowed uninhibited, touching every curve and crease.

She caught up with Cate and, in silence, they swam towards the line of buoys that marked the boundary of the Lido on the Serpentine water. She could just make out the outline of Cate's head and her arms holding the line of buoys. She could hear the water lapping against her as she moved.

'This is amazing.' Cate sounded close and intimate. This private moment was as far away from other people as it was possible to be in London. The dark sky stretched over them down to the soft shapes of trees on the bank, not an onlooker in sight. They seemed insulated from the rest of the world, the water and night sky enveloping them.

'It's difficult to believe we're in London,' Pia said in awe.

She saw the outline of Cate's head nod. 'I've swum in the Maldives and the Red Sea surrounded by desert, but this is somehow more remarkable.'

'So this will do for your tropical swim under the stars?'

'It will more than do, Pia.' Cate's voice was low and sensuous, as tantalising as the warm water that touched Pia's body. 'It's wonderful.'

Pia breathed out, seduced by Cate's tone. She blushed, wondering if Cate knew the effect her words had on her. She kicked out her legs in the water and tried to act unaffected. Pia hooked her arm over the rope and turned to the bank. But as she swept around, her arm slipped past Cate's firm nipple.

The sensation of being stroked by Cate's breast sent a thrill of pleasure up her arm and through her body. She almost gasped at the sensation and held her breath to keep control. They floated motionless in the water, the lapping sound from their movements receding until all they could hear was the distant hum of the city.

Pia was aware of her pulse pounding through her head, and every inch of her sensitive skin crying out to be touched. Her head buzzed with longing and she prayed that her body remained under her own volition and didn't reach out to touch Cate.

She heard Cate swallow and clear her throat. 'Come on Benitez-Smith.' She sounded strained. 'You owe me dinner.' And she heard Cate ripple through the water back to the shore.

6

'What do you fancy?' Pia asked.

They strolled away from the lake towards a wide lit path. Cate shivered. Her wet hair hung in dark ribbons around her shoulders. 'Something comforting,' she said, rubbing her bare arms.

'Hold on.' Pia stopped and shrugged off her rucksack. She drew out a cropped denim jacket and held it around Cate's shoulders. 'I hope you don't mind something a bit more high-street.' She giggled as she covered Cate's couture dress.

'Not in the slightest. Thank you.'

Pia pulled out her phone and tapped the screen. 'OK, I think I know what would fit the bill for dinner.'

'Not a restaurant in Knightsbridge I imagine.' Cate nodded towards the Kensington Road.

Pia smiled and shook her head. 'No. I had a food truck in mind, but I need to check online where they've parked up tonight.'

Cate opened her mouth and then breathed out. 'I'll suspend my judgement,' she said. 'You've surprised me more than once tonight.'

'Southbank.' Pia switched off her phone and turned in the opposite direction. 'It's quite a walk in bare feet or high heels, so I think I'll treat you to a ride on the Underground.' She grinned at Cate and offered an arm.

Cate laughed as she encircled Pia's arm with her fingers and they headed across the park.

They sat beside one another on the bench seat that ran along the side of the Tube carriage. Pia studied Cate in the dark reflection of the window opposite, interrupted by infrequent flashes of light from the tunnel lamps. Cate sat in a refined posture, her elegant legs crossed and her hands clasped in her lap. In comparison Pia's reflection was dishevelled, a brush with foliage and a dip in a lake taking their toll.

Even with the slight distortion of the curved window Cate was beautiful, her high cheek bones and eyes more defined in the dim light. Pia didn't know how long she'd been staring when she noticed Cate's eyes had locked on hers. Pia twitched away at first, but then returned her gaze.

Cate started to turn, her nose elongating in the warped window. Pia giggled. Cate twisted more, her nose resembling a mendacious Pinocchio. She stuck out her tongue so that it seemed to stretch almost to Pia's ear.

Pia laughed out loud and covered her mouth. An elderly lady further down the carriage glanced up from her eReader. She didn't look disapproving, but Pia stifled her laughter until the woman returned to her read.

Pia tilted her head and noticed another version of herself upside down in the window above her reflection. She tilted up her head until her brow stretched to meet the inverse twin, so that her two heads were joined in a ludicrous hour glass shape. She heard Cate trying to suppress a snigger.

The woman along the carriage put down her eReader and smiled at them.

'I have to ask,' she said in an accent that wouldn't have been out of place in a 1950s BBC. 'How long have you two been together?'

Pia's reflection opened two mouths in surprise.

'We're not together,' Cate said, her tone generous and amused.

'Really?' The woman caught Pia's eye.

'Oh God no,' Pia said, embarrassed for Cate that someone would assume that they were a couple. 'In fact, I've no idea who she is.'

Cate laughed. 'We met a few hours ago.'

The woman's deep wrinkles stretched as she raised questioning eyebrows. 'Well.' She sat back in her seat. 'Whatever you two have, they should bottle it.' And she turned back to her book.

Cate and Pia giggled as they stepped on to the platform. They walked arm in arm towards the escalators.

'Do you reckon she...' Pia gestured back towards the Tube.

'What?' Cate grinned.

'You know.' Pia nodded her head back. 'Do you think she was a...'

'A what?'

'Oh you know,' Pia whispered.

Cate leant in. 'Are you trying to say lesbian?'

Pia was a little piqued. 'I do know how to say it. I perhaps thought. Well I thought she might be. I can't imagine many older ladies would assume we were a couple. So I thought, maybe?' Pia shrugged.

Cate stopped, her expression incredulous. 'Pia. Of course she was.'

'Oh.'

'A good old girl with a pair of slacks like that. She has to have a companion somewhere in Stoke Newington.'

'Wow. I can honestly say that passed me by.' They turned and ambled on.

'What do you think she was reading?' Cate's tone was mischievous.

Pia rolled her eyes. 'Oh, something like *The Well of Loneliness*.'

Cate shook her head, 'No, I think she had a bit more spark to her than that. I think she was more of a lesbian erotica person.'

Pia's jaw dropped. 'You are much naughtier than you first look.' She started to think. 'What do you reckon? *101 Ways With Lube on the Tube?*'

'I think that lady was far beyond instruction manuals. I'd go for erotic stories.'

'*Lizzie Pays Lip Service?*' Pia suggested enthusiastically.

Cate began to giggle.

'*A Pussy's Wet Tale?*' Pia guessed again.

'Actually dear, you're not far wrong.'

The perfect newsreader pronunciation stopped Pia and Cate in their tracks. They swung round to see the elderly woman, striding behind them.

'*Spank My Mistress. Dyke Domination 3.* I can recommend them whole-heartedly.' She smiled and marched past, her eReader tucked under her arm.

Pia and Cate stared in unison after the woman who hopped onto the bottom of the escalator and was swept out of sight. Pia felt Cate shudder next to her with laughter. She couldn't help but join her and the two dissolved into giggles.

———

When they emerged from the Tube station, an incessant stream of text messages and missed calls chimed from Cate's clutch bag. They wandered across Charing Cross pedestrian bridge, trains rattling by in the caged rail track that ran alongside. Pia could feel Cate's mood sinking as they walked above the swollen waters of the Thames, swirling in eddies beneath them.

Pia gazed down at their entwined arms. She wondered how it had been that she'd spent the night with such a beautiful woman. Cate was clearly meant to be on a more refined evening than Pia could ever show her. It made Pia feel odd, thinking of Cate in elegant society. She imagined her in a ballroom with men in black tie and ladies in gowns, mingling with ease, a sophisticated crowd that was far beyond Pia. She imagined Cate joining them and a twinge of jealousy pinched inside. She held Cate's hand tighter to savour the last moments before she knew she must leave.

'Do you need to go?' Pia whispered.

Cate drew her lips into a tight line. 'Just a few more moments,' she said. 'Let me see what you had in mind.' She quickened their pace, their arms locked together and they descended the steps onto the broad walkway of the South Bank.

It was busy with summer evening entertainment. Artists drew chalk versions of classic paintings on the pavement. A juggler played with fire. Animated couples chattered as they left the Royal Festival Hall from concerts, exhibitions and films. The book market was open late, its tables of paperbacks laid out beneath Waterloo Bridge. People huddled around, enjoying the act of browsing as much as they would reading the books.

'Here it is,' Pia said.

They stopped by a large vintage Citroen van, its corrugated sides painted in perfect glossy blue. Inside the long hatch was busy with people, flipping over crepes to feed eager customers who waited outside rubbing their hands.

Pia inhaled the warm aroma of buttery pancakes that steamed out of the van. 'French crepes and hot Italian coffee.'

'That sounds perfect,' Cate breathed.

They sat on a wall overlooking the river, their feet hanging above the water. Pia devoured the folded-up crepes. The syrupy lemon dripped through her fingers onto her paper plate. Cate licked the buttery sugar from her fingers and Pia giggled at her obvious enjoyment.

Pia hugged the fresh coffee to her chest. She inhaled the strong roasted vapours and sipped the scorching drink. The hit of coffee filled her mouth and nose and she gasped out with satisfaction. 'Why does food taste so much better when you're outside?'

'And after an invigorating swim,' Cate added with a smile.

They were silent for a while. Cate looked away across the Thames to the flickering lights of the Houses of Parliament downstream. Pia allowed her to have her peace and watched a ferry chopping through the waters.

'Do you want children?' Cate asked.

'Bloody hell, that's quite a question.' Pia spluttered.

'Sorry it is, isn't it? I just wondered.'

'Because I'm gay and it's something you have to think about more if you're gay?'

'Perhaps.'

'Do you want kids?' Pia asked.

'I don't know.' Cate looked troubled. 'I think I did. You see, I was always made aware of how much trouble I was to my mother. And I've never met anyone who wanted to have children with me.'

Pia was lost for words. She couldn't think why someone wouldn't want to have a family with a woman like Cate.

'It's so difficult,' Cate continued. 'All those trade-offs. Do you find someone who's your best friend, or your best lover? Someone rich, intelligent, who wants the same as you, or someone who wants a family?'

Pia remained quiet. She had never thought of it like that. She thought that when she met the right person it would feel right.

'What about you?' Cate said. 'You didn't say if you wanted children.'

'Oh, I would love kids.' Pia beamed. 'Always have.' She put her hands either side of her thighs and kicked out her feet in enthusiasm.

'What kind?' Cate asked.

'Stripy ones.'

Cate laughed. 'I mean, do you want a boy or a girl?'

'Don't care. Happy healthy ones. Lots of them.'

Cate seemed caught up by her enthusiasm. 'I always pictured myself having two boys. I don't know why. It's one of those fleeting images you sometimes have when you picture how your life might be. It's my first thought when someone says the future.'

'Would that make you happy?'

'Yes it would,' Cate said, lifting a sad smile to Pia, her watery eyes sparkling in the streetlight.

'What else is in your future?' Pia found herself more than a little interested in Cate's ideal life.

'Do you mean in that fleeting image?'

'Yes,'

'I don't know,' Cate said, an expression of surprise and confusion on her face. 'I can't see anything else. But I'm happy. I'm content and it's not just because of the boys. There's a feeling of security and love.'

'From a partner?'

'Yes. I think it is. It's strange I've never thought about that before.' Cate's face lifted with fond realisation. 'Yes. I'm content. I can't see them, but there's someone in the background I love and trust. Someone who makes me feel good about who I am. Someone who makes me happy.' She turned back to Pia, her face full of wonderment.

Pia's face flushed with happiness. 'That sounds like a wonderful life.'

Cate's eyes searched Pia's. 'I'd like very much to—'

A message alert, loud and harsh, interrupted their conversation. Pia's feeling of warmth slipped away as they stared at Cate's glowing phone. Cate tapped the screen. The light was extinguished and the phone was silent. But a chill had settled. Without speaking, Cate handed back the denim jacket and Pia folded it away. They swung their legs around and dropped down to the pavement.

49

Pia's chest felt like it might implode. Cate stood before her, her face full of reluctance and sorrow.

'I have to...'

'I know,' Pia whispered.

Pia didn't know what to do: revel in the exhilaration that the night had been or cry now that Cate was leaving for good. She shuffled and pushed her hands into her pockets, torn between reaching out and holding Cate tight or offering to shake hands in somber farewell.

'You have given me an incredible evening.' Cate's voice was quiet. 'Better than any I could have planned for myself.'

Pia couldn't respond. She stared at her feet, her stupid feet that wouldn't stop shuffling like an awkward teenager's. She felt Cate's soft fingers touch her cheek, enticing her to lift her face. Pia didn't dare catch Cate's gaze and she closed her eyes. Cate's full lips caressed her cheek in a soft kiss, just close enough to the crease of her mouth for her lips to tingle with desire.

'Goodbye,' Cate whispered and Pia heard footsteps click behind her and recede down the river.

Pia heaved with strained breaths. She willed herself not to turn around, fearing her heart would break if she saw Cate walk away.

'Oh God.' She covered her mouth with her hand. She felt nauseous that such a woman was walking out of her life.

'Start walking,' she commanded. 'Don't look back. Walk.'

She concentrated on one step at a time. One heavy left foot and then the right. The walkway filled with people. Blurred silhouettes emerged from the bright lights of the Festival Hall. The air filled with excited post-concert chatter, and animated figures buffeted Pia, dazed in the flow.

The streetlights, dark figures, jugglers and buskers were a bright and noisy blur. She cowered in the harsh atmosphere of pleasure. Her throat began to choke. With every step she felt the loss of Cate heavier inside. It was only now that she realised how close they had become in such a few vivid hours. The thought that she would never see her again strangled her. Her breaths were short and harsh. Hot tears threatened.

And then she felt Cate's soft fingers slip between hers.

'Come with me,' Cate whispered.

Lightness flooded through Pia. Her legs buzzed with energy and felt as if they could float. Wide-eyed with awe she watched Cate's figure walk ahead, and trembling with anticipation she let her sweep her away.

7

They stumbled through the balmy night, following the river along the tree-lined avenue. Cate never let go of Pia's hand. The touch of their bare arms was tantalising and Pia's heart thumped with anticipation.

Cate didn't say a word, not even when they turned off the Strand down a side street. Pia's heart raced that bit quicker when she saw the Savoy Hotel, its golden statue with shield and spear presiding over the grand canopy entrance.

Cate released her hand and was swept inside through ornate rotating doors. Pia followed and tripped into the great hall. She watched Cate glide across the chequered floor to reception, and stared around the hall, her mouth open wide.

It was like an old glamorous film, perhaps a setting for an Agatha Christie story. Well-heeled guests dotted the leather sofas waiting for their spouses, and murmuring couples in evening wear disappeared out of view into a soft-lit bar. Pia spun around in the middle of the generous room, taking in the details, until her eyes locked with those of the doorman's.

He stood to attention under his top hat, his lips curled in a smile beneath his moustache. 'Forgotten your luggage?'

Pia didn't have time to blush before she felt Cate's fingers around her arm. She looked back once to see the doorman wink and she was whisked away.

Cate rattled the key in the door to the Monet suite, peered around the corridor and led Pia inside. The door clicked behind them and they stood in darkness. The city glowed outside, the lit Ferris wheel of the London Eye across the river peeking in through the window.

Cate's body was dark in the middle of the sitting room. Pia reached out, tentative, her sight not yet adjusted to the room. Her fingers brushed against Cate's forearm, and she stroked down her skin to find and hold her hand.

'You're shaking,' Pia said.

'It's been a long time since I slept with a woman,' Cate whispered.

Pia clasped Cate's hands, squeezing them with gentle reassurance. Together they edged towards the bedroom, the same view glimmering through the window. Neither said a word as they stopped by the bed. Its sheets lay smooth and inviting, waiting for them.

Only their hands touched. Cate's face and body were indistinct, but Pia could feel her warmth, that sensation of someone near wanting to be closer still. She could hear Cate inhale, her gasps shallow but quick with excitement. The silhouette of her slim shoulders rose and fell with longing breaths.

Pia drew near. Cate's sigh was moist on her skin. She could taste her as they breathed into one another. Their lips touched, and the excitement of that first intimate sensation shot down her neck, through her chest and breasts. She closed her eyes as Cate's lips slipped hot over hers. They kissed deeply and Pia salivated at the sensuous contact.

With reluctance but necessity she drew back, enough for their lips to part. She reached up to Cate's dress and unclipped the strap from around her shoulder. The material fell fluidly from her, caressing every curve as it fell. Pia stared down at Cate's naked body, the soft light touching her full breasts, her slim belly in shadow. With the lightest of touch, Pia slipped her fingers around Cate's white underwear which yielded and dropped to the floor.

She stared into Cate's dark eyes, as she stripped off her own T-shirt, jeans and underwear and stood before her, exposed and expectant.

They stepped together at the same time. Their breasts touched for a moment and she heard Cate's sharp intake of breath. Pia stroked around the curve of Cate's hips and drew her close. Slowly their breasts touched and sealed together. The delicious sensation rippled around her whole body, the hair on her back tickling to attention.

Cate's lips kissed her forehead, covered her eyelids, moved down her cheeks, urgently seeking Pia's. She opened her mouth to receive Cate who licked her inside.

She could feel Cate's nervous desire as she caressed her back, exploring her skin with her fingertips and pulling her closer. Their legs slipped between one another. Cate's pubic hair tickled her thigh and arousal fluttered inside when she felt the moisture there.

She ran her fingers down Cate's body, enjoying the full touch of this wonderful woman. She wanted to savour her, but her hands were impatient. She stroked her fingers down, through Cate's hair, and teased along the top of her legs. She touched her hair in achingly slow circles above her clitoris. Cate quivered with every teasing stroke and Pia could feel her pushing herself into her playful hands.

'Touch me,' Cate whispered. 'Please touch me.'

Pia pulled Cate's body tight and with delicious and complete enjoyment, slipped her fingertip between Cate's lips. Cate's body tensed rigid at the touch. Her clitoris was swollen and firm. Pia's fingers touched round and round, feeling Cate's clitoris and enveloping lips inflame.

Cate's urgent panting gave away how close she was. Pia moistened at Cate's sensuous and erotic response. She could smell Cate's fresh sweat and moisture, warmed by her aroused body.

It was almost involuntary, the strong compulsion to kiss Cate's breasts and down the line of her stomach. She guided Cate towards the bed and sat her at the edge. She knelt down and gently touched her face to reassure her.

'I want to kiss you,' she whispered.

Cate's gasp was all the sanction she needed. Pia enticed her legs apart. She leaned down to nuzzle around her hairline, her head beginning to daze with Cate's scent. Pia licked at her wet hair enjoying her taste and flicked her tongue around Cate's lips.

Cate trembled, as if the slightest touch would take her over. Pia hesitated, enjoying the fragrance once more and the feel of Cate's smooth thighs around her face. And then she opened her mouth and kissed Cate's clitoris.

Cate groaned and thrust herself forward. Pia pulled her tight to her face. She kept Cate's clitoris squeezed between her lips as she came, licking her tenderly as her orgasm seized her.

Delirious with arousal, Pia half registered Cate lift her face and take her arms. Gentle and expert hands manoeuvred Pia to the bed. Practised lips teased around her breasts and Pia moaned as the teasing became firmer and Cate nibbled her.

Fingers caressed down her stomach. Greedy kisses sent pulses of excitement through her body. She was beyond thought when Cate's tongue parted her hair and slipped deep inside her.

She arched her back and cried out. Cate clasped her breast, pushing her into the soft sheets. The sensation of her breast being squeezed with passion and Cate's mouth sliding up to lick her clitoris triggered the first waves of her orgasm. Cate pushed her face deep into her moisture and Pia closed her eyes as the surge of pleasure and tension gripped her body and consumed her thoughts.

Disoriented in the darkness and hazy with the flood of hormones, she was only half-aware of Cate caressing her way back to her. Uncontrolled and clumsy, they kissed and wrapped their limbs around each other in a tender, satiated embrace.

They roused in the middle of the night. Loving hands reached out and bodies entwined to make love again.

And it was still dark when Pia thought she heard Cate whisper: 'You gave me quite the surprise Pia Benitez-Smith, and I don't think I'll ever recover.'

8

Pia woke in a peculiar state of both clarity and confusion. The room was bright and sharp with morning sunshine and the white walls dazzled her. She didn't know what had woken her, but she had switched from pleasant slumber to alert in an instant. She checked around the bedroom. She knew Cate had gone, but she didn't know why and where and whether she would see her again.

As she stared at the incomparable view of the Thames and London skyline, she realised she was in shock. She had never thought she would achieve her dream of staying at the Savoy and a night of passion with a woman so extraordinary. But now, she wasn't certain that the woman of her dreams hadn't been just that.

She rubbed her fingers through her short hair, which stuck up with an impressive mix of tree, lake and Cate. Pia covered her face with her hands and rubbed her eyes. She sighed at the wonderful aroma that scented her fingers. Certainly not a dream.

As she came to from its euphoric effect, she stared half-focussed at the rug. A piece of white card, torn at one edge, came into focus. When she picked it up, she recognised it as a business card. 'Catherine Gillespie' was written in bright blue ink next to a silhouette of a woman's head and a company name of 'Bennet'. She swept over the card for a telephone number or email address, but that half of the card was missing, and the small typed letters that teased at the frayed edge were a string of 'x's. On the back was scrawled a note: 'What do you think?' Even more confused than before, she dressed and slipped the fragment of card into her jeans pocket.

The hotel entrance bustled with guests leaving or making their way to a late breakfast. Pia shuffled through and hesitated by the reception desk. Should she check that Cate had paid? A flutter of apprehension agitated her chest as she thought about the cost of a Thames-view suite at the Savoy.

'You wouldn't be thinking of doing a runner would you?' a deep voice said behind her.

When she turned round, the doorman smiled at her from beneath his moustache, with the same twinkle in his eye as the night before, although he looked a great deal more tired.

'Um. I. Don't know if I. Might not have enough…' Pia stammered.

'It's all right love. She paid before she left.'

Pia held her breath, her pregnant questions threatening to burst out. When did she leave? Was she all right? Did she leave an address or telephone number? She looked from the doorman to the receptionist, frustrated that they had the answers, but were unable to tell her.

'The course of true love never did run smooth,' the doorman said, raising his eyebrows, and he bid her farewell with a kind wink.

Pia wandered dazed through the noisy weekend streets, almost missed her stop on the Tube and emerged in Brixton some unknown time later. Her body knew the way home and it took her on automatic out of the Tube station and along Electric Avenue.

Little by little the market street's assault on her senses broke through to her consciousness. The sounds of reggae, hip hop and soul all mixed in the narrow street. She passed fresh fish stalls with whole specimens staring out glassy-eyed. The fusion of pungent exotic fruit and vegetables warmed by the sun lifted her mood. As she detoured through Brixton village, the mix of faces, cultures, ages and classes welcomed her home. She was smiling when she reached the door of the small terraced house that she shared with her mother.

The smell of chorizo and smoked paprika lingered cold in the air from last night's dinner.

'Shit.' Pia rushed through the cramped sitting room, out into the tiny kitchen and through the open door into the garden. 'Mama?'

She ducked under the arbour, dodging the swollen bunches of grapes and tendrils of soft leaves. She peered around the small garden. It was bursting with runner beans, trailing squash that clung to the fences and tomato plants that looked so big they could walk off into a science fiction film.

'Mija? Is that you?' Her mother's voice, heavy with accent, called from the back of the garden.

Pia pulled back a large silver artichoke leaf and found her mother on a bench. All middle-aged motherly curves with streaks of grey lining her chestnut hair, she was attending a small orange tree in a pot.

'Mama, *lo siento.*'

Her mother crossed her arms and glared. Pia skulked under the vegetation.

'You didn't have time to send your mama a message? Couldn't tell her that you wouldn't be back for your favourite home-cooked dinner?'

'I'm so sorry Mama. I completely forgot.'

'Hmm. What made you forget your old mama, heh?

Pia blushed and stuttered, 'I. Kind of. Met someone.'

'Oooo, mija.' Her mother's change in mood was instant. 'Come tell me,' she said and she patted the bench beside her ample bottom.

Pia slumped down, not reluctant to talk to her, but perplexed about what had happened.

'I met the most amazing woman, Mama.' Pia stared into the garden, not focussing on anything. 'She was beautiful, elegant, kind, funny.' An image flashed into Pia's head of Cate sitting on the bed, her legs apart. She flushed at the thought and sighed. 'Oh God she was amazing. Perfect.'

'I am so pleased,' her mother said, drawing out the words. 'So, when you going to meet this chica again?'

'I don't know.' Pia shook her head.

'You don't know?'

'I don't have her phone number.'

'You meet the perfect woman and you don't get her phone number,' her mother said with disbelief.

'I know. It's all a bit odd. I've even seen where she lives. But I know that she doesn't want me to contact her. She wasn't once interested in calling me. It's so confusing.'

Her mother drew in air between her teeth. 'Be careful mija. She sounds trouble.'

'No. She wasn't like that.'

'Mmm hmph.' Her mother's scepticism hummed through her lips and whistled out of her nose.

'Really. She was bright and generous. She's a very kind person.'

'Beautiful too, heh?' Her mother sounded suspicious.

'Oh God yes. Damn it. There was something so special about her.'

Her mother put her hand on Pia's knee and gave her a gentle squeeze with her plump fingers. 'Pretty girls will do that to you.'

Pia felt dejected. She peeked up at her mother who gave her a naughty grin in return, perhaps wanting to cheer her. 'Come on,' her mother said nudging her. 'What was so special about this chica?'

'Oh, where to begin?' Pia sighed.

'Did she have great titties?'

'Mama!'

'Like melons? Big water melons?' She held two armfuls of air in front of her already generous bosom.

'No, no, no, no.' Pia covered her face.

'Or just a nice handful, like a pair of oranges?' Her fingers squeezed the air with gusto.

'Mum! No.' Pia stuck her fingers in her ears. 'La la la la la.'

Her mother laughed and pushed her shoulder. 'Mija. I'll stop. I know when you call me Mum I push you too far.' She fell quiet but left a consoling hand on Pia's shoulder. 'So what was it? What's got you all gazing at the stars?'

'I don't know. She was just... She had...'

'That certain something.'

'Yes.' Pia nodded with enthusiasm and exasperation.

'Oh, I know that one. I know it well little one.' She squeezed her shoulder. 'She must have had her reasons mija.'

'But it felt so right. In my dreams right. I thought she felt the same way.'

Her mother tilted her head. 'Sometimes real life has a habit of getting in the way of dreams. Perhaps it does for her. It does for almost everyone.'

Pia implored her mother. 'It didn't for you.'

'Perhaps.'

Pia's phone beeped. She snatched it out of her pocket in the impossible hope that it would be Cate. She was disappointed to find another message from her agent, but news of the sale of her photograph to the daily newspapers began to warm her belly.

'I sold a photo Mama,' she said smiling.

'That's good. How much did you get?'

'Three thousand pounds so far.' Her grin broadened.

'So much money for one picture?'

Pia blushed not wanting to admit that she had taken it not altogether legitimately. 'It was a good picture Mama and, if I can top up my wages like this, I can take that staff job at the magazine.'

Her mother frowned.

'Please Mama. I'm trying to make a living from this.'

Her mother gave her a sad smile. 'I know. I prefer you had a good normal job. I just want to keep my little girl's feet on the ground, so she doesn't fall with a bump. And it's better you concentrate on this than on some woman who doesn't have the good sense to give my little Pia her phone number.'

—

And Pia did try to follow her advice, with varying degrees of success. She accepted the post as staff photographer on a new magazine, and spent the week readying herself for the dream job. She bought a secondhand Vespa for travelling to assignments and, at the insistence of her mother, a brand new helmet. She took to the streets after rush hour to familiarise herself with the scooter's handling while the London traffic wasn't quite its most belligerent self. And more than once her practice route took her close to Kensington. And it wasn't unknown for her to take a sheepish ride through Kensington Square, keeping her gaze straight so she didn't take an impertinent peek into Cate's flat.

After two days, she tapped 'Catherine Gillespie' into a search engine. The hundreds of results showed women of all shapes, sizes and ages, but none who resembled Cate. Another search for 'Bennet' yielded hundreds of websites devoted to *Pride and Prejudice*, insurers, bars, but nothing resembling the silhouette logo.

Every night, she kissed her mother who gave her a look of sympathy and squeezed her cheeks. She smiled a little, unable to hold cheerful eye contact, and moped up the stairs.

In bed, she took out the torn business card and stroked the worn surface where Cate's hands would have touched. She lifted the paper to her cheek and was transported back to the hotel room. She could feel Cate's touch. Her body remembered how her fingers had caressed and it tingled at the memory. She could recall Cate's smell and the way she sounded; the way she said Pia's name with that fond mischievousness. It played over and over in her head. She stroked the card one last time, staring at Cate's name spelled out in full, and tucked the treasure back in her wallet.

In the mornings she greeted her mother with a cheery 'good morning' and pretended she wasn't preoccupied. She assumed it was successful. But by the end of the week, one dinnertime, she was still distracted.

She leaned on her elbow, staring down at her mother's comfort soup, Sopa de Ajo. Even that was unappetising, and she prodded the poached egg around the bowl.

'Mija. Enough.' Her mother frowned at her across the tiny Formica table. 'I don't mind you sulking around the house for days, but when you waste my food something has to be done.'

Pia looked up with her mouth and clueless eyes wide open.

'Go call on her. For god's sake knock on her door. Leave her a note. Something.' She threw up her hands.

'Do you think I should?' Pia started to grin and rise out of her chair.

'No, but I think you have to.'

'Oh,' Pia said, and she sat down again.

Her mother reached across the table and squeezed her hand. 'I don't think she wants to see my lovely Pia again, crazy woman. But I think you need to hear it from her.'

Pia deflated a little more.

'Go Pia. Put your mind at rest. For better or for worse. I'll be here when you get back.'

Pia beamed. That tiny grain of hope, the fraction of a possibility that Cate might want to see her, was enough to fill her with energy and joy.

'Go. Shoo.' Her mother waved her arms at her. 'I don't want to see you again until you've talked with her.'

Pia sprinted from the house, leapt on her Vespa and spluttered into the night. She felt high as she weaved through the traffic, giddy with excitement at doing the thing she'd avoided all week but wanted most in the world to do. As she turned into Kensington Square, her heart pounded so hard that she could feel it in her throat.

She locked the scooter to the railings around the garden, the chain clinking in her trembling hands. For a moment she peeked up at the residence of the immigration minister. Or to be more accurate, the ex-residence of the ex-immigration minister, after both his wife and political party had washed their hands of him. Her agent had bungled her name, but the photographer 'P. Smith' was now well-known in news circles.

But, as they had been all week, Pia's thoughts of Cate were uppermost. She followed the same path Cate had taken from the garden and stopped at the corner where the road exited the square. She stared at the small art gallery, its windows dark after closing time. Its door and one to the side were the only ones Cate could have entered. Pia scanned the residences above. All but one of the five floors were dark.

Pia's nerves and anticipation threatened to overwhelm her. There was still a chance that Cate's was the apartment that was occupied. Numb with fear of rejection and burning inside with hope, Pia stepped up to the doorway. She ran her fingers along the name tags, deciding which button to try first. The lowest two floors belonged to the art gallery. The next label, which corresponded to the lit floor, showed a Mr and Mrs Adamczyk. And there at the top, the last possibility, was a blank label.

66

Pia stood frozen, her finger hovering over the doorbell. With an involuntary action she pressed it. She thought she could hear an echoing ring from above. Nervous, like a naughty child, she stepped back and stared fearful at the top room.

No lights came on. No-one pressed the intercom to invite her in. She stepped back further and further across the road, and when she stood on the pavement opposite she spied the To Let sign plastered inside the window.

The disappointment sank cold into her belly, and she looked away feeling more than a little foolish.

'OK Cate. I get the message. I'll stop now.' Pia drew out the tattered business card one last time. She rubbed its smooth surface with her fingertips and then stretched out her hand over a black litter bin. She turned away not wanting to watch and tried to drop the card.

She stared down at her hand that was reluctant to let go, unable to throw Cate away. She snatched it back, and held the card to her chest.

'Just a memento,' she whispered. 'That's all.'

9

With her tummy in her mouth and legs like a gelatinous dessert, Pia walked with awe along Fleet Street. It was difficult not to be impressed by the old law courts, countless monuments, buildings that survived the Great Fire of London and modern monoliths with preserved mediaeval pubs hidden in their basements. The giant dome of St Paul's loomed over all.

Pia grinned with excitement as she climbed the stairs to her dream job on the top floor of an old press building. When she pushed open the smart double doors into reception it wasn't quite the slick office she'd imagined. Cardboard boxes, half unpacked, lay on the floor. An electrician was having words with the wiring and a light that flickered. And all she could see behind the reception desk was a large round bottom, covered in stretched black material and sticking up in the air.

'Err...good morning?' Pia said.

A whole person flipped up from the bottom, with a red face and mass of streaked curls.

'Oh hello my darling.' The receptionist pinched her frizz back into place. 'What can I do for you?' She shuffled into a seat and adjusted her large breasts so the bottom half settled into her bra. Pia politely lifted her gaze away from the other half that threatened to explode out of her top.

'I think I have a job here,' Pia said.

'What's your name love?' She chewed the words over a piece of gum and stretched it across her tongue. She started to flick through a list on the reception desk.

'Pia!' A confident male voice boomed across the reception area. Pia recognised the proprietor from her interview. She had supposed him to be in his forties when he'd worn his pin-striped suit, but he looked younger today. He flicked back hair that had flopped across his face and jogged across reception in slim red jeans, a polo shirt and cardigan. He stuck out his hand, and she noticed the new deep tan on his arms.

'Rafe. Just call me Rafe.' He spoke with same East End accent as the receptionist, which seemed at odds with his image.

'Hi,' Pia said. She grinned while Rafe squeezed and shook her hand with vigour.

'Great to see you. This is so exciting,' he enthused. 'Ton of things to do this morning, as you can see, but we'll have a kick-off meeting and presentation in a bit.' He squeezed her shoulders with his hands, and Pia felt like she'd been captured by a well-meaning vice. 'I was so impressed with your portfolio. It's magic you can join us.'

'I'm so pleased to be here.' Pia beamed. 'I can't wait to start.'

'That's what I like to hear. Lots of enthusiasm. The whole thing's going to be pukka. You'll see.' And he ruffled her hair. 'Right, I'm going to leave you in the capable hands of Denise. But you must catch up with Edith ASAP.'

He left as quickly as he'd arrived and Pia and Denise stared at the whirlwind of energy that disappeared down the corridor.

'Dreamy isn't he?' Denise stared longingly at the space that Rafe had occupied. 'So nice as well. Do you know he's royalty? In line to the throne, one hundred times removed.

Something like that. But you wouldn't know it from the way he talks with everyone.'

Pia nodded, having found him very pleasant in the interview, but her admiration not extending much further than that.

'Married, of course.' Denise sighed. 'Just back from his honeymoon.' And she tutted, descending back to planet Earth, 'Anyway my darling. You're quite early. There's only you and Edith so far. You'd better go and talk to her I suppose. She's down that way.' Denise stretched out her arm and squashed her breasts over the reception desk. 'Follow the gnashing and snarling noises.'

Pia glanced at Denise perplexed, but the receptionist rolled her eyes, slipped off her chair and stuck her bum in the air to continue unpacking.

Pia crept in the direction Denise had indicated, listening out for the tell-tale sounds. She wound around tables, chairs, computer screens in bubble wrap, all strewn in the corridor. All she could hear was the sound of a vacuum cleaner. The offices were open and empty except one with a scrawled note taped to its door proclaiming 'Ed'. It was from behind this door that the vacuum cleaner noise growled.

Pia knocked on the door. She tried louder with her knuckles. Then she pounded it with her fists. The vacuum cleaner wheezed into silence.

'Christ, just open the door. Don't break it down,' a voice shouted from the other side. It was one of those authoritative and well-spoken voices that could have commanded hell to freeze over.

Pia peeked inside in time to see the woman stub out a cigarette. The dying smoke lingered in a trail up the tube of a vacuum cleaner wedged in the window.

'Oh lord. Which one are you?' The woman raised her eyebrows above the straight black lines of her glasses. She was tall when she stood up, six feet at least. The wild grey flicks of her hair added another inch. 'Well. Which pint-sized journo are you then?' She placed her hands on her hips.

'Pia. I'm a photographer.'

'I'd forgotten the silly tit hired a staff photographer. Well you're here now,' she said, extending a hand and business-like shake. 'Name's Edith, but don't ever call me that. God awful name. Call me Ed.'

Pia was shaken by another forceful personality.

'Right then shortarse. You'd better tell me a bit about yourself.'

Pia bristled. 'I'm not that small.'

Ed replaced her hands on her hips. 'When we both stand, all I can see is the top of your head. You're short. Now sit down. It'll make you more comfortable if you can look me in the eye rather than the bust.'

Pia complied, piqued but secretly amused by the exchange.

'Right, in case you don't know, I'm the editor of this new rag. As such, it would have been nice if Mr Just Call Me Rafe had let me interview the handful of permanent staff that I'm going to torture.'

Pia couldn't help but smile.

Ed continued. 'I mean really "Just Call Me Rafe". What the bloody hell else does he expect us to call him? Lord Rafe of Faux East End?'

'I thought he was a distant relative of the royals or something?'

Ed rolled her eyes. 'Yes, a very distant relative of the old girl. Bet you don't hear her saying "Just call me Liz".'

'He doesn't speak as if he's posh,' Pia said.

'That fake East End accent? Pathetic isn't it? He wants to appear like the common man. Your average geezer. But the man's worth a fortune. He would have to be to set up something as cretinous as a new magazine in this climate.'

'I thought he owned several magazines and was doing well?'

'Yes he does darling. He's very ambitious, and to his credit he's done well spotting gaps in the market.' Ed puffed out, exasperated. 'I heard the twit say he wants to be the new Rupert Murdoch. Only someone obscenely power hungry or irredeemably stupid would have an ambition like that. I'm tempted to say the latter. Well at least he hired a nice little baby dyke for me.'

Pia took a moment to realise that Ed meant her. She pouted and snapped, 'I'm not that young.'

'How old are you dear?' Ed peered over her glasses.

'Twenty-four.'

'That's neonatal to an old dinosaur like me.'

'Well you don't seem that old to me,' Pia spat.

Ed opened her mouth for a riposte, but closed it again and smiled. 'Nothing so disarming and charming as honest flattery. Well done shortarse. Well done.' She considered Pia further. 'Perhaps Just Call Me Rafe knows what he's doing.'

'I quite liked him,' Pia admitted.

Ed inhaled and gazed out of the window. 'Well,' she drew out. 'I've got to say he must be a little bit of a romantic, basing his offices in Fleet Street. It's been a bloody long time since I've worked here. Couldn't move for hacks back then. Those were the days.' She had a distant look in her eye. 'Yes, maybe he has the one redeeming feature. That and his gorgeous wife.'

—

Pia shuffled into the conference room with Ed's breasts for company. They were the last inside and squeezed against the back wall. Obscuring their view were men in suits, journalists in jeans and bemused middle-aged women in overalls.

'Who are all these people?' Pia whispered, 'I thought it was a small team.'

'It is. But the investors are in today. He wants it to be a good show,' Ed scoffed. 'I recognise some of these hacks from his other rags. He's even dragged in the cleaners. Cheeky bastard.'

Pia stretched up on tip-toes and peeped over the shoulders of a tall man blocking her view. She could see Rafe standing at the front, readying himself for a speech. He turned back every so often to people seated beyond Pia's view.

'Shall I lift you up?' Ed said. 'Put you on my shoulder?'

Pia frowned at her, not knowing whether she was serious. 'No,' she said, incredulous.

'Seriously I could darling, a small scrap like you.'

'Bugger off.'

Ed laughed a throaty smoker's chuckle.

'Ladies and gentlemen,' Rafe shouted over the hum of the crowd. 'It gives me great pleasure to welcome everyone today.' People ceased their conversations and after the hush of shuffling feet, the room went quiet.

'Out of all my publications I'm most excited about this one,' Rafe boomed. 'Everyone loves gossip. When you're at the dentist, doctors or hairdressers, I bet every one of you picks up that copy of *Heat* or *Hello*. We love it don't we? But some of us don't want to be seen reading them, and some don't want to admit to liking them.

'So we're going to give people a quality gossip magazine. We're going to titillate them with all the juicy bits about their favourite TV and art-house film stars. We're going to tell them about Stephen Fry's latest diet and all those things they read in the online *Daily Mail* when no-one's watching. Then we'll slip in the odd serious in-depth interview to make them feel better about enjoying all that other stuff.'

Ed rolled her eyes at Pia.

Pia was surprised. She whispered skywards at Ed. 'Don't you think it's a good idea?'

'Oh yes, I think it's a damned good idea. Wouldn't be here otherwise. I just wish he wouldn't be so crass about it all.'

'Now,' Rafe continued from the front. 'This all needs to be presented with care, and I'm not the one to do that.' The crowd murmured and some sniggered. 'So my team of designers with a brief from my wonderful wife and my new editor,' he nodded towards Ed who waved above the crowd, 'have been working on the magazine's image and logo.'

Ed leaned down. 'Well at least he had the good sense to delegate. His wife is fantastic to work with and a bloody good journalist. Award-winning writer on *The Times*. God knows how he persuaded her to defect here. Must be love,' she muttered.

Rafe continued. 'We wanted the name of the magazine to resonate with all those who have good taste. And after checking with an expert,' he turned to grin at someone behind him, 'we came up with Mrs Bennet — *Pride and Prejudice*'s supreme gossip. So after a bit of brain storming with the team,' he ducked down so that Pia could no longer see him. 'I'd like to present you with simply *Bennet*.'

He held up a large card with the name 'Bennet' in large blue letters and the silhouette of a woman's head. It took a moment for the large version of Cate's business card to sink in. Pia stared at it and her brain flooded with thoughts and questions.

The designs were identical. Pia's heart pounded with excitement at the implication. She snapped her gaze around the room, over the shoulders of investors, underneath the armpits of applauding writers. Every glimpse of a strand of blonde hair sent a thrill through her.

'So while I'm at it.' She half-heard Rafe. 'I'd like to introduce our star journalist, poached from *The Times*, Catherine Hammond.'

Pia started clapping along with the crowd as she scanned around.

'Now my wife, Catherine Gillespie.'

Pia chilled in an instant, Rafe's words an icy bucket of cold water. With disbelief she stared at him. Her heart thumped while she held her breath, wishing it not to be true. Then she heard Cate's unmistakable silky voice.

10

Pia was transfixed by the sight of Cate. It was shocking to meet the woman with whom she'd been so intimate as a different person. She was serene and beautiful although pale next to the tanned Rafe. She turned to him with a wide smile, except this one didn't reach her eyes. Pia couldn't reconcile the expression with the woman who had laughed and loved with her.

'You all right shortarse?' Ed said. 'You've gone as white as my derrière.'

Pia came to. Her cheeks flushed with blood and humiliation. 'I'm not feeling great. Sorry. I need to get out of here.'

She wanted to leave the room before her emotions broke through. The speeches over, people pushed past on their way to the door, and Pia and Ed were pinned to the back wall. Tears threatened and Pia gulped trying to keep her turmoil inside.

Rafe's voice shouted out. 'Edith. You should have been up there.'

Pia tried to push her hands through the crowd to escape, but Rafe was already upon them.

'I wanted to introduce you to everyone,' he said.

'Bit late to the party I'm afraid,' Ed replied.

'Well I see you've met Pia at least. That's great.'

Pia edged round. She held her breath and peered up with dread.

Rafe beamed at her. His arm was stretched back to Cate's hand. She was a step behind, finishing a conversation with another employee.

'Well while you're here,' said Rafe. 'Let me introduce you to my wife. I haven't told her yet, but I think you two would make a great team. This is Cate.' He gestured back, and gave Cate's hand a gentle tug. 'Cate, this is our photographer, Pia.'

Cate hadn't been paying full attention, flicking her gaze between Rafe and the person she was bidding farewell. But at the mention of Pia's name, she snapped round.

Cate looked stunned. She stared, unblinking, at Pia. Pia shuffled and averted her gaze. She cleared her throat, and when she looked back Cate was beginning to compose herself, but was clearly not ready to speak.

'How do you do?' Pia said. She felt like she was going to choke. She put out her hand and almost recoiled when Cate's cool fingers clasped hers.

'I've heard great things about you,' Pia managed to say. Still Cate was silent. Pia blanched again and felt sick.

'You do look a bit peaky darling,' Ed said. 'Are you all right?'

She couldn't look any of them in the eye. 'No. I'm not feeling well. Please excuse me.' And without a glance back she ducked away into the crowd.

Pia joined the flow of bodies, her chest heaving with emotion. The crowd swept her away from the humiliating scene. She was released into reception and she ran as far as she could down the corridor to a small vacant office.

She stumbled inside and stared in disbelief out of the window. Below, Fleet Street was a blur through the first tears. She tried to control her breathing to stop the shuddering inhalations from descending into full blown sobs.

'Pia?' Cate's voice was quiet.

She could see Cate's reflection pale in the window. Pia sniffed and swiped away a tear. She crossed her arms and turned round. Cate didn't approach and hesitated in the doorway. She looked pained, but that was of no comfort.

'Pia. I'm—'

'I should have known.' Pia cut her off with an unsteady voice. 'I should have guessed that you were married.'

A mix of shame and sorrow cast across Cate's face.

'I knew you didn't want to see me again.' Pia said, her voice shaking. 'You didn't once show any interest in where I lived, or how to contact me.'

'I would have found Pia Benitez-Smith,' Cate murmured. 'There aren't many of those in the world.'

Her reply confused Pia for a moment. It sounded as if Cate had thought of contacting her. Even now, that kindled a glimmer of hope inside her. She flushed, embarrassed at her desperation. Tears threatened again as reality flooded in. 'But you didn't,' she whispered. 'Because you were married.'

'I nearly—'

'Or you were about to get married.' Pia frowned and stared at Cate. She thought through Rafe's speech and the introduction with Denise. Back from honeymoon? His new wife? 'My God. That night? Was it your hen party? The one you were avoiding?'

Cate blushed and didn't meet her eye.

'Christ,' Pia said. 'Did you marry him the next day? On the Saturday? The morning after our night together?'

Cate coloured deeper and kept her gaze averted.

Pia reeled back. She rubbed her fingers through her hair and shook her head. Her thoughts and impressions of Cate were in turmoil. Her image and love of the warm and kind woman she'd met that night began to sour. Cate's expression seemed to plead. Pia thought she understood Cate's intention and her anger burned.

'Look,' Pia snapped. 'I won't say anything, if that's what you're worried about.'

'That's up to you. That's not why I came here. But if you do tell him, please, not in front of anyone. Don't humiliate him.'

'Of course I wouldn't. I think he's a nice guy.'

'He is a nice guy.' Cate said it matter of fact, with neither fondness nor regret. It wasn't something Pia could respond to. A tense silence hung between them. Pia stared at her, blood pounding in her ears and cheeks burning. She wanted to say a thousand things. A hundred things to shout at her, a hundred more to hurt, and as many questions filled her head. But the words stuck in her throat and she didn't even know if she wanted to hear the answers.

Cate's eyebrows crinkled with concern. For a moment, Pia's anger subsided, allowing her empathy to reach out and wonder at Cate's feelings. She didn't look guilty. She wasn't begging for her infidelity to be kept secret. She looked hurt and, if anything, as if she wanted to comfort Pia. But the memory of Rafe introducing her as his wife intervened and anger rose up again.

'Whatever's going on with you two is between you two. I'm not going to cause any trouble. I hope you sort it out.'

Cate didn't respond and Pia hugged herself tighter. The silence made the humiliation all the more excruciating. With thoughts fighting in her head, Pia stepped forward to leave.

'I want to get out. Please. Excuse me.'

'Pia...'

Cate reached out to touch her but Pia snatched her arm away.

'How could you do that?' Pia spat, her fury getting the better of her. 'Just how could you touch someone like that?'

And she meant it in every single way. How could Cate caress her with tender kisses along every curve of her body? How could she run delicious fingers between her legs, and mesmerise her with those adoring eyes that moved her so deeply it made her heart beat quicker than any physical touch?

She glared at Cate. 'How could you touch someone like that? And marry someone else in the morning.'

She stared for a moment longer, her anger burning as fresh tears, and pushed out of the room.

—

Pia paced in front of old Brixton Prison with its austere walls of unhealthy-coloured brown bricks. She checked her watch again and glanced towards the tall wooden doors. Other people loitered nearby, waiting for visiting hours. A small door within the main doors opened and visitors filed through, trying not to appear as if they were either carrying something or planning something.

She spotted her father as soon as she walked into the visitors' room, his small wiry body sitting alert by one of the tables. He stood up and gave her that incomparable look of love, admiration and support that no-one else could give her.

'Oh Dad.' The tears threatened again. She threw her arms around his neck and squeezed him as he rocked her back and forth.

'Hello my lovely girl,' he whispered in her ear. He stroked her hair and held her tight. Her resolve faltered and tears flowed warm over her face.

'Hey come on now.' He squeezed her tight. 'Let's sit you down. Otherwise the screws will get twitchy and think you're handing me a spade to dig out or something.'

She giggled and then sniffed a very wet sniff. She wiped her nose and the tears from her cheeks.

'Come on. Sit yourself down.'

They held each other's hands in the middle of the table.

81

'I'm going to take a wild guess,' he said. 'It's this woman your mama's been telling me about, isn't it?'

Pia nodded, her mouth pulled down. 'Oh Dad. She's married.' She sniffed and wiped her nose on the back of her hand.

Her father raised his eyebrows in sympathy so that his brow creased into tens of deep furrows. 'It did sound like it might be something like that from what your mama said.'

'Well, she didn't tell me.' Pia sulked.

'She didn't want to rub it in.' He squeezed her hand. 'So you've seen this woman, this Cate again have you?'

Pia nodded.

'And she's happily married?'

Pia shrugged. 'I assume so. She's just back from her honeymoon.'

'Ooo, ouch, that sounds like bad timing.'

Pia took her hands away and dropped them dejected into her lap. 'I feel so stupid. I thought she was special, and for her it was some easy last fling.'

'Was it? Your mama said it sounded like you had a truly romantic evening.'

'Did she?' Pia was surprised and hopeful all at once.

'Oh your mama talks all sensible and practical, but she's a big soft romantic deep down.' He grinned. 'Why do you think a good old Catholic girl with conservative parents doesn't bat an eyelid when you bring a woman home?'

Pia shrugged in a sulk.

He reached out and wrestled her hands back into his. 'After all the trouble we had being together, we both swore to never stand in the way of our children and the people they loved. No matter how surprising.'

'Was it a surprise? Was she surprised?'

Her father shook his head. 'Nah. Looking back, we knew when you were two years old. You were a right little tomboy.' He laughed and then his face slipped into a more serious expression. 'This Cate, did she make excuses, try to brush you off?'

'No. No she didn't. She was very considerate in a way.'

He regarded her for a moment. 'Trust your heart Pia. Always trust your heart. It'll know what to do.'

'Well, my heart hurts.' The pain returned as she said the words.

He gave her a sad smile and nodded. 'Let's hope you can forget her then poppet, and let that heart recover for someone else special.'

Pia shook her head. 'They don't get that special. And it's difficult to forget someone when you work with them every day.'

'Ah.' He sat back smirking and crossed his arms. 'That's why you've come to see your old dad.'

Pia didn't understand.

'I'm guessing that you've come to me to tell you to stay in your job. If you wanted someone to tell you to leave, which would be very sensible I might add, you would have talked to your mama.'

Pia was torn between giggling and desperate frustration. 'It's my dream job. Staff jobs don't come up for people just out of college.'

Her father nodded.

'So you think I should stay,' she said, the enthusiasm returning.

He frowned. 'Can you work with her, without hating her?'

'Maybe.'

'Are you still holding a candle for her?'

Pia couldn't answer.

'Because if you are, you are going to get burned all over again.'

'Oh now you sound like Mum,' she said exasperated.

'Oh dear, she has annoyed you hasn't she? Calling her Mum.'

Pia chuckled and they were silent for a while. They exchanged a fond look.

'Don't give up this job Pia,' he said. 'You worked so hard at college. The first Smith to go to university. I'm so proud of you my darling.'

Pia blushed at her father's compliment, and the privilege of university that her father had never had.

'You've got such a good eye,' he said. 'Don't you give up. You don't want to end up like your old man, trying this, that and the other, hating all of it and messing up big time. When you get it right your photos capture someone's soul.'

—

The sound of water running in a washbasin in the ladies' room trickled into Cate's consciousness. There was no other sound. She was insulated from the office, Rafe and London. She leaned on the bank of washbasins with her head down. The marble top was cold beneath her palms except around her finger where her wedding and engagement rings pinched. Rafe ensured she wore them now. She flicked them round with her thumb, still not used to the way they felt.

She lifted her head to face herself in the mirror. Her complexion was pale despite walking for hours in the heat of the London streets trying to contain the feelings and conflicting thoughts that Pia had so vividly stirred.

'How could you touch someone like that?'

She could hear Pia's voice as she remembered the words that trembled with anger and hurt. Cate's eyes became hot, and a heavy teardrop tickled her eyelashes. She blinked to spread the tears thin and checked her appearance in the mirror. Her eyes were glassy and she inhaled long and hard trying to suppress the beat of her heart and swell of emotion.

'How could you touch someone like that? And marry someone else in the morning.'

The words were debilitating. Every time they surfaced her blood would chill. Her arms shook with tension. She snapped her hands away and stood straight.

'Enough,' she chastised. 'Enough of this.'

She lifted her chin and stared at her image. Filling her lungs and pulling back her shoulders, she forced herself back into whom she was meant to be. She spread her lips into a polite smile, which she'd been wearing since the wedding, and turned on a heel to leave the room.

Through two sets of doors, the seclusion and silence changed into clamour and chaos. Men in overalls hung a company logo above the reception desk and employees carried computers to offices. A group harangued the receptionist and Rafe and Ed bickered in the centre of the room.

Rafe spotted Cate as soon as she entered. The firm diplomatic expression that he wore in disagreements flickered into anxiety and he drew away from Ed.

'I'm not finished Rafe,' Ed said.

Cate saw him force patience and he resumed the conversation as Cate drew towards them.

'Honestly, where did you find the child photographer?' Ed continued. 'Lovely little thing, but is she always going to be this flakey?'

Cate flushed, realising they talked of Pia. She held her breath and prayed her heartbeat would subside as she approached them.

'Like I said,' Rafe retaliated, 'have a look at her portfolio. I don't think you'll be questioning her talent after that. It knocked my socks off.'

'It's all very well taking pretty photographs, but I need her to be in the right place at the right time, and right now I'm buggered if I know where she is.'

Rafe turned exasperated as Cate joined them.

'Ah Cate,' Ed said. 'Thought you'd gone AWOL like a certain other recruit. You don't happen to know where young Pia is do you?'

Cate shook her head and hoped her voice was controlled. 'Perhaps she's gone home if she was feeling unwell.'

'She'd better be at death's door. I won't excuse her disappearing like this Rafe.' Ed threw a warning glance his way. 'I need to brief her and I won't hesitate to kick her perfect little behind out of the office if she slopes in late tomorrow.'

Ed turned to leave and guilt shivered through Cate. She'd broken Pia's heart, and now she was losing her a dream job.

'Ed, please,' Cate said.

Ed swirled around. 'Heavens, not you as well?' She frowned when Cate failed to continue. 'Well? Pray tell me why I should keep Pia?'

Cate had been about to say how moved she'd been by Pia's photograph of joyful children playing on rough ground. It had showed the finesse of a much more seasoned photographer and talent of only a few. But she realised she should never have seen that shot. She should never have met Pia before that day. Nothing about Pia Benitez-Smith should have touched her deeply. Words of any use failed her.

'Give her a chance please,' she stuttered. 'If Rafe says she's good.'

Ed raised an eyebrow and her expression exuded disappointment. 'Hardly convincing Ms Gillespie.' And Ed resumed her unimpressed exit.

Rafe blew out a long lungful of relief. 'Thanks for backing me up.'

Cate pinched her lips into a smile of acknowledgement.

He peered at her, apprehensive. 'Where have you been? I haven't seen you for hours.'

'I had to make some phone calls.' She tried to reassure him. 'It was chaos here so I thought I'd clear up a few loose ends out of the office.'

He stared at her with the same concerned expression. 'Is there anything I need to know?'

Cate glanced down out of reflex but, resolved that there was little more to be gained, peered up. 'There's nothing else Rafe.'

She reached out and enticed his large fingers into hers. 'Let's go somewhere quieter.' And she led him away.

11

'Arse,' Pia said. She hadn't even opened her eyes. 'Arse,' she repeated.

Pia sprang up in bed and rubbed her eyes. It was early morning and the rising sun shone bright through the thin curtains of her bedroom. The red numbers on the digital clock showed an hour much earlier than she needed to be awake.

'Oh God.' She hung her head in her hands. 'Why was I such a tit?' Her cheeks became hot behind her fingers as she blushed at the scene in front of her new colleague, Catherine Hammond.

'Why couldn't I have been a bit more cool about it? Just a little bit.' She peeped out between her fingers not sure she could face her own reflection in the bedroom mirror today, let alone the woman she had been spurned by, her new husband and an intimidating boss.

The small slice of room she could see between her fingers revealed her bedside table and phone. She snatched it up and brought up a browser. Whereas Cate Gillespie had been a fruitless search, Cate Hammond yielded far more interesting results.

The woman featured in the top entries was without a doubt Pia's Cate. The first article included a glorious photo of Cate beaming with joy at the British Press Awards. She had won Investigative Journalist of the Year. Scrolling down, Pia found an entry on Wikipedia and feasted on the information on Cate's double first at Cambridge, her quick succession of posts at increasingly prestigious newspapers and her reputation as a determined and scrupulous journalist.

Pia blushed and sank into the bed as she read on. She remembered her indignation at Cate and felt a little foolish and more than a little inadequate as she read of Cate's accomplishments. The last article she read announced her engagement to the billionaire Rafe Gillespie, by all accounts a suitable match.

She tapped off the phone and sagged into the mattress. 'Bugger.' She closed her eyes and wished she was someone else and somewhere else, but the confrontation with Cate tortured her by replaying in her head. A little time later, the beep of her alarm broke her self-induced torment, and she reluctantly slid out of bed.

'OK. Time to face the music.' And she dragged herself to work.

—

The office was a different place this morning. A glossy sign for *Bennet*, big, bold and blue, hung above reception. Curving white chairs reclined around the waiting area and the side offices chattered with activity. This was all no doubt achieved through the boundless energy of Rafe, who indeed bounded over to Pia at that moment.

'Pia! Good to see you.' He put a strong arm around her shoulder and squeezed her under his wing. 'I was worried about you, rushing off like that.' Beneath his flopping, salon-cut fringe he looked genuine in his concern.

A pang of guilt and embarrassment shot through her. It was no wonder that Cate had chosen him. He was handsome; even a devout dyke like Pia could tell that. Tall, amiable, charismatic, bit of an idiot, but very rich and successful. Small, pretty novice photographers from

Brixton, with a propensity for accidents with trees, weren't that much competition.

'I'm fine now, thanks,' she said, and she tried to smile.

'Great! Let's get you to Edith. There's work to do.' He squeezed her tight and accompanied her the whole way. His chest was firm against her shoulder and he enveloped her in his warmth. His male smell was mixed with spice and musk deodorant and a strike of jealousy reminded Pia that this was how Cate must feel in his arms. An image of them naked together flashed in her mind, Cate's soft breasts against his muscular torso. She imagined Cate responding to his touch. She could hear her breathless arousal, the memory of it still vivid. It made her nauseous and she was glowering by the time Rafe delivered her to Ed's office.

Ed and Cate sat around the desk laughing.

'Ah shortarse. About time. Sit,' Ed said, amusement still vibrating in her voice.

Cate's expression dropped. She attempted a smile but looked at Ed as if to avoid further acknowledgement.

'Right,' said Ed. 'I've got the chaps and chapesses trawling the news feeds and agencies for suitable fluff to fill the first edition. But what the hell am I going to do with a rookie photographer and an award-winning writer?'

Pia blanched, already feeling inadequate.

'Don't knock Pia,' Cate said. 'She's a bloody good photographer. Remember that Michael Haywood photograph last week?'

'What, the immigration minister sacked for assault, or "On Yer Bike Mike" as *The Sun* put it?'

'The very one.'

'That was you? You're P. Smith?' Ed's eyebrows shot above her glasses. 'Well, brava shortarse. I'm impressed.'

Pia nodded and her lips twitched at the compliment, but Ed didn't let her bask in the acknowledgement long.

'This, however,' Ed continued, 'is going to be more tricky. I hate to admit it, but Rafe the gentleman editor may have hit upon a good idea with you two.' Cate frowned mock disapproval at Ed. 'I think you'd make a great team for some of the more substantial editorial pieces. So buddy up and swap telephone numbers. You're going to be spending some time together.'

Pia shuffled, uncomfortable in her chair.

'I would have briefed you both yesterday, but one of you had an attack of the vapours.' Ed glared. 'So. Is everything all right now?' Ed stared at Pia like a formidable headmistress and Pia had no choice but to nod. Ed turned the look on Cate and elicited the same reaction.

'Good.' Ed leaned forward onto her desk. 'I want you two down at the London Fashion Show today. Not one I'd usually cover, but word has it that the design team for David Quick has had a hissy fit and walked out.' She sighed. 'All because he wants to use the odd large-size woman to model the collection. And by large-size he means slim to normal.' She rolled her eyes skywards. 'God forbid that they show clothes on someone who might wear them. Hate to think what they'd do if they were from the right age group too. But anyway, with a temporary design team running the show it should be even more chaotic than usual and a perfect chance for some backstage gossip.'

She flung two passes at them over the desk and continued.

'So you.' She squinted at Pia. 'I want people with thighs rather than sticks, please. And pictures of Judi Dench or that Mirren woman looking gorgeous in the audience. That should keep everyone happy. Cate, please schmooze and ooze and extract some juicy details please. Someone's bound to be misbehaving. Everything clear?'

'Crystal clear,' Cate said.

'Any questions?'

Pia shook her head.

'Good. You need to prove yourselves. Now, go stir.'

And Ed turned her attention to photographs on her desk and didn't glance up to see them out.

—

They walked in silence down Fleet Street. Cate glided with perfect posture. She wore a pale, slim-fitting dress that wouldn't have been out of place on the catwalk. A small black bag swung over her arm and her face was half-hidden behind sunglasses that sealed the exclusive look. Pia shuffled alongside, wondering if she should have borrowed something other than her jeans and T-shirt. Her large shoulder bag for her cameras and lenses clunked by her side.

She peeped at the elegant woman beside her. The more she learned of Cate and saw her in the light of day, the more Pia felt out of her league. But the hurt still wouldn't heal.

Cate peered down at Pia, a gentle expression on her face. 'We can talk, if you like.'

'I'd rather we didn't,' Pia muttered, her pout returning in an instant.

Cate stopped. She reached out and curled her fingers around Pia's arm. 'I really think we need to Pia.'

Pia snatched her arm away like a child in a tantrum.

'Look,' Pia snapped. 'I know it was just a last fling for you, OK. So I'd prefer not to go over it. I'd rather we stuck to work things.'

Pia stared at the pavement but, from the corner of her eyes, she could see Cate watching her. Her expression was pregnant with emotion and thought, but she didn't reply.

'Just work things please.' She peeked up and attempted to make it less personal. 'This job means a lot to me. I already made a tit of myself yesterday in front of Ed. I don't want it to happen again. She's judging me on what I do today.'

Cate still held her arm. Pia hadn't felt the slightest waver in her grip and still she watched from behind those sunglasses.

'Can we just get to Somerset House?' Pia said. 'Please.'

She saw Cate nod and her arm fell away limp. They started to walk, and the sound of their footsteps was a welcome break from the silence.

The set for the fashion show occupied the entire grand court of Somerset House. The catwalk was hidden inside a daunting black temporary building with mirrored sides. Pia snapped pictures of journalists, models, show audience, all checking their appearance in the reflections.

Cate led them around to an entrance reserved for crew and models, and as soon as they entered the air exploded with music, anguish, screams and laughter. A large man in a black T-shirt examined their passes and nodded over to the backstage area.

It seemed like chaos to Pia. Stations for hair and makeup were a flurry of activity. Three people at a time transformed a thin, pretty woman with healthy, enviable locks into a black-eyed zombie with dry bird's nest hair. Assistants rifled through jangling clothes hangers and thrust rails across the floor to the next desperate colleague.

'If you wanted the credit for using fat fucking models,' someone shouted above the clamour, 'why the fuck didn't you make fat fucking clothes?' Pia turned round to see a statuesque woman hurling a thread of a dress across the room.

A small man, rubbing his forehead, emerged from the crowd.

'Oh darling!' he said when he saw Cate. 'It's such a disaster.' They embraced without touching and the man kissed the air by Cate's cheeks three times. 'Thank God this is the rehearsal.'

Pia watched as Cate slipped into conversation. She smiled at the right times, made the right compliments to stroke his ego, was admired when he stood back to adore the outfit she'd chosen. They were joined by a well-dressed woman, barely able to lift her jewellery-laden arms, who showered them with pleasantries and empty flattery.

It was a distant world. Pia watched Cate as if she were in a film. She was a different character from the woman she'd first met. Cate tilted her head and laughed with her mouth open wide at jokes Pia didn't understand. Cate glanced back to Pia to beckon her into the auditorium and Pia obliged without a word.

Pia lost count of the number of times Cate waved across the assembling audience to the shriek of recognition from someone recognisable by everyone. Pia snapped away at the crowd, capturing the rising sense of excitement. Public figures from every sphere peppered the photos.

A renowned actress took her seat without fuss and responded to shouts of greeting with humble waves. Pia zoomed in and grinned as she captured the distinguished actress holding glasses to her eyes with one hand and her phone distant from her face with the other. In an instant, delight wrinkled the actress's face, in the way that everyone loved. Pia saw her mouth form the words: 'Oh my dear. How lovely to see you'. She threw her arms around a woman's shoulders and when Pia zoomed back she saw that the other woman was Cate.

Through the lens she saw Cate lean back in a chair and roll her eyes. The actress grinned and patted her knee. They huddled together, chuckling in private, and without realising Pia took photo after photo. Cate leaning forward with her hair caressing her face. Cate peering up, her breasts soft and visible down her dress. Now laughing without restraint, with that beautiful smile that creased around her eyes.

Pia checked the last photo and zoomed in on the camera screen. That was the smile. That was the one. Her body filled with warmth, glimpsing again that wonderful woman from a perfect night. She twisted the camera round and admired the shape of Cate's high cheekbones augmented by her spontaneous joy. Pia didn't think she'd ever seen such an attractive combination of mature, elegant beauty and soft youthfulness in a woman.

Cold reality sank inside her, leaving an emptiness from admiring something that wasn't hers. 'We're in different circles,' she whispered. She flicked through the photos once more, mournfully admiring Cate's unattainable grace.

'The show's about to start.'

Cate's voice made her jump and Pia snatched the camera to her chest.

'How are you getting on?' Cate asked.

'Fine.' Pia was short and still clutched her camera.

Cate regarded her for a moment. 'Pia, I'm not checking up on you. I wondered if you needed anything. I'd better go and get my place and take notes.' And without a smile she left.

Pia kicked herself for overreacting and being rude. Cate's interruption had been a timely reminder to change the camera for one with a more suitable lens.

The show was starting. Someone killed the lights and the arena plunged into darkness. The audience murmured. People shuffled and whispered, disconcerted when the spotlights didn't come on.

The opening to *Carmina Burana, O Fortuna* blasted out of the speakers and reverberated around the arena. The pitch black still shrouded everyone and Pia thought she could hear someone screaming when the music subsided to a whisper.

A dim glow appeared at the back of the stage. The whispering of the choir accompanied slender models with hollow faces. They tip-toed unsure down the catwalk. The dim runway lights twinkled alight with their passing footsteps.

Pia started to shoot with her zoom lens from the pit below the catwalk. The tentative choir grew louder as more models crept along the runway. The tension in the crowd was palpable. People whispered, in between admiration and anxiety, and all the time the music built to a crescendo.

The sudden crash of the bass drum thundered around the arena. Full stage lights struck like lightening. The crowd gasped, but drew breath sharper still when twelve full-bodied women marched onto the stage.

Six-foot models with six-inch heels stormed the runway with attitude. They were models with hips, thighs, shoulders that could lift a woman and breasts that could smother her. Not even the zombie look could diminish their presence. Pia kept snapping, grinning like an idiot as the powerful women blasted onto the catwalk.

The music approached its climax. By instinct, Pia grabbed another camera with a wide-angle lens and shot almost without looking, clicking away on both cameras.

The models lined the edge of the runway and, defiant, faced the crowd as the drums, brass and choir all peaked in one lasting, mighty note that blew the audience away. The orchestra and lights plunged into dark silence and the audience erupted into applause.

12

Still grinning from ear to ear, Pia rushed backstage to photograph the manic scenes. The costume changes, from hanger to model, were almost instant. The whirlwind of models and stylists swept through to the next collection. Pia stumbled back and slumped onto a pile of clothes. For a few moments she sat with her chest heaving trying to catch her breath.

Also slumped behind a rack was a model. Her eyes had the smudged look of the previous set and Pia gave her a polite smile. When she heard a sniff, she realised the woman was crying and that's what the panda eyes were a result of.

'I'm sorry.' Pia scuttled beside her. 'I thought it was just the makeup. I didn't realise you were crying.'

'S'ok.' The woman swayed a little.

'Are you OK? I mean I know you're not OK and you're crying. But are you feeling OK?'

The model inhaled, shuddering with tears, and slurred, 'Shitfaced.'

'Oh. Oh dear,' Pia said. 'Erm. Don't you need to be modelling clothes or something? How much have you had to drink?

The model held up a Champagne glass.

'One glass of Champagne?' Pia said, incredulous.

'Wrecked. Kicked me off the show.'

'What's happened? Why did you drink, erm, so much?'

'My boyfriend's left me.' Her mouth pulled down at the corners in a cartoon extreme and dribble stretched out of her mouth. 'And he's taken Archie.'

'Oh God. How horrible.' Pia assumed Archie was her son and, being delicate, didn't seek confirmation.

The model stalled into a stuttering cry, her arms flapping by her sides. 'I...miss...him.'

'Of course you do.' Pia reached out to comfort her and pulled her close.

'I really, really miss him.' The model sniffled on her shoulder. 'I miss his little furry face.'

'Of course you.... Sorry. What did you say?'

'His furry face and his cute little whiskers.'

Pia squinted skywards while still hugging the model. 'Who is Archie by the way?'

The model opened her mouth as another wail convulsed through her. 'My raaaaaaaat.'

Pia gave the model a good squeeze. 'I'm sure it'll be OK. I'm sure he'll bring him back.'

The model sniffed beside her ear. 'He's the sweetest thing you've ever seen. Siamese little fella with brown paws and a cream body.'

'He sounds...special.' Pia tried to be understanding.

As the model dribbled and sobbed on her shoulder, Pia came to the realisation that this was the kind of opportunity she was meant to be taking advantage of: a vivid example of the insanity backstage that would impress Ed. Pia's heart sank with the prospect of ridiculing the fragile model in a gossip magazine. She thought about reaching for the camera, but her fingers were numb and wouldn't move. Her lips curled as if to a nasty taste in her mouth.

She sat the model up and checked towards the opening of the stage. It flashed with cameras out in the arena. If Pia didn't take advantage of this woman, there'd be others who would.

'What's your name?' Pia asked.

'Elana,' the woman had difficulty saying.

'Well, I think we should take you home Elana,' Pia said, and a ripple of familiarity stirred in her consciousness.

'Go and tell,' Pia thought she heard the model say.

'Go and tell?'

The model slurred with some urgency. 'Go and tell!'

'Go and tell who?'

The model shook her head and slumped forward over Pia's lap. She'd said 'Going to hurl', but Pia only heard that in retrospect.

Tepid liquid seeped through her T-shirt onto her belly. The same moist feeling seeped through her trousers and onto her thighs. For a woman who'd only had a glass of Champagne, the amount of liquid and coverage was impressive.

'Oh,' Pia exclaimed. 'God.'

'I'm so sorry.' The woman wiped her mouth and a small trail of sick into her hair.

Pia stood up and pinched her clothes away from her skin. The smell was overpowering and Pia feared breathing. She shuddered and peeled away her jeans from her sticky legs and wriggled out of her T-shirt. Her clothes landed with a wet slap on the floor.

Standing in her underwired bra and tight white boxers, she flicked through the garments on the rails. She found a dress, she assumed, made of matchsticks but couldn't fathom which limb went through what hole. She found a sensible black gown, but the inbuilt feather balaclava was perhaps too conspicuous for smuggling out a model. Besides, full-length garments made for models were impractical for a petite Pia owing to the two feet of spare material that gathered at her feet. The next item was a short dress that appeared to be made of plastic beer-can rings.

Pia muttered, 'You'd think there would be something to wear at a clothes show.'

The beer-can rings might have been impressive on a model, but Pia brought a new level to them, one closer to a bag lady's.

She snatched up a silver wig for herself and a blue version to drape over Elana's hair and face.

'It's going to have to do.' Pia tutted.

She picked up her bag and supported a wobbling and babbling model on her shoulder. 'Let's get out of here, while everyone's still in the show.'

Pia stared at the floor as she limped along under the weight of her bag and the model. They'd taken a couple of short paces when two slim legs with elegant shoes appeared before her.

Pia peeped up. She recognised the pale dress above the knees. She recognised the long fingers placed over the hips. And that chest she would never forget.

Cate's lips were tight in a horizontal line and she frowned at Pia.

'What's going on?' Her tone was softer than Pia anticipated.

Firstly, she was disappointed that Cate recognised her, and secondly she was also very aware of how ludicrous she looked. She imagined that she resembled an extra from a bad science-fiction film with an incoherent alien for company.

'Do you know who this is?' Cate said.

'Elana,' Pia said, missing the all-important emphasis in Cate's sentence. 'I don't know her surname.'

'It's Devanka. This is Elana Devanka.'

Now that she heard Cate say the name without the drawn slur, that nagging feeling of recognition from earlier became crystal clear. The dribbling woman on her shoulder was a supermodel, a regular in the daily newspapers.

Without a flicker in her expression, Cate continued. 'So why are you kidnapping the world's most highly paid supermodel, and stealing several thousand pounds worth of designer clothes?'

Pia hadn't thought of it like that and, not for the first time that day, and it would never be the last, she felt rather stupid.

'She's been sick,' Pia said.

'Yes, I can see that.' Cate frowned and came forward. She crouched down and peered at the model who'd closed her eyes and was swaying. 'What's she taken?'

'She said she only drank this.' Pia nodded to the empty glass on the floor.

Cate considered for a moment. 'Possible I suppose. Look at her, she's so skinny a small glass of Champagne is a leg full.'

It took a moment for Pia to realise that Cate was joking.

'So what are your plans?' Cate raised an eyebrow.

'I was going to take her home,' Pia said, embarrassed to be smuggling out their biggest story of the day.

'Yours or hers?'

'Hers.' Pia was serious, still a beat behind Cate's humour.

'Right,' Cate said. Pia slumped, expecting to be ordered to take photos for the magazine or kiss her job good bye.

Cate ducked under the model's other arm. 'We'd better not get caught Benitez-Smith.' And they both dragged the multi-millionaire model from the scene.

Pia and Elana emerged from the black box of the arena and glittered in the sunshine. Panic gripped Pia's belly. They looked ridiculous. They may as well have had a neon arrow pointing at them. Around the entrance hung suspicious stylists sneaking a quick fag. Tourists stopped and stared.

Cate glanced at them with an anxious expression. 'I'll flag down a taxi. Hurry up.' And she skipped ahead across the court.

'Here.' Pia heard someone say. 'Isn't that what's her name?' People were starting to point as Pia and Elana stumbled towards the archway.

'It is innit,' someone else replied.

Pia tried to pull Elana's wig further over her face, but they weren't going to escape attention. Two eager young women ran towards them. They giggled and fumbled with their phones.

'Oh bloody hell.' Pia was desperate. 'What are we going to do?'

'Get a drink? I'd love another glass of bubbly,' Elana slurred.

Pia tried to drag the unhelpful Elana at a greater pace but they weren't going to outrun two young fashionistas.

'Stay back!' Pia said. She took a moment or two to think about her next step. 'Erm. Can't you see how ill she is?'

The joy dropped from the faces of the two women. They stared at Elana's pale complexion and dark eyes.

'It's... she's got...' Pia was about to warn them that Elana had contagious winter vomiting virus, but that was particularly unseasonal. Bird flu also suffered from the same lack of veracity. So she started to panic. The two women were regaining their composure and interest. Then she said, very earnestly, with great authority. 'Plague. Can't you see? It's the plague.'

The two women glanced at each other. Pia expected them to burst out laughing and brush her aside to take photos. But they backed away. They looked terrified. With horror stretched on their faces they babbled to each other in Polish and, when a few feet away, they twirled and fled from the courtyard.

'Oh.' Pia was quite shocked by the efficacy of her diversion. 'I wonder what they thought I meant.'

For a moment, the hysterical tourists distracted other onlookers. Pia put her head down and made a last big push for the street. Cate sat waiting in the back of a black cab and dragged Elana in. Pia leapt after, her silver locks flying in the breeze, and the clunk of the door sealed them inside.

'Drive,' Cate shouted. And, after a few more stern words to the cab driver, where Cate threatened removal of various organs that hung external to the body, they made lightening progress through the afternoon traffic.

—

They soon arrived in an exclusive Chelsea street. Elana yelped when she peeped out of the window. Outside her immaculate multi-million pound house sat a returned and relieved boyfriend and an overjoyed rat. The boyfriend was met with tears of joy, the rat was given an unrestrained kiss and smooch and Pia was showered with profuse words of gratitude.

Pia had to pull herself away from the grateful trio. When she turned back to the taxi, Cate was smiling at the reunited family. Her expression faltered when she saw Pia watching, and she withdrew as Pia settled back in her seat.

'Brixton please,' Cate ordered in a neutral voice.

They both sat in silence staring at the perspiring neck of the cabbie as he drove south of the river. Pia shuffled her feet and crossed her legs draped in plastic threads.

'Well,' Cate sighed. 'So much for intrepid gossip reporters.'

Pia blushed and folded her arms. Cate's eyes flicked down to Pia's chest, and then she averted her gaze. Pia hadn't appreciated that her arms would push her breasts out of her bra and squeeze them through the plastic rings like bizarre and huge bubble wrap. She dropped her arms in disgust. When would the humiliation end?

'I did include me in that statement by the way,' Cate said.

Annoyed with herself, Pia regarded Cate. She was still that beautiful woman she'd first met, but the more she found out about her the less she seemed to know.

'I don't understand you,' Pia whispered.

Cate watched her, but didn't say anything.

'You worked for the *Guardian* and *Times*. You covered social affairs and exposed scams in government and industry. You were tipped to move to the *New York Times* as a section editor.' Pia blushed as she realised she was betraying her internet research of Cate's background. 'You reminisce about studying English, and the beauty of Cambridge. Then you marry some rich capitalist and drop everything to work on a gossip magazine.'

Cate twitched at the last accusation.

'Everyone needs money Pia.'

'Some more than others,' Pia muttered.

Cate breathed in. 'It's fine to live like that when you're young. To have ideals like that.'

'But you're not much older than me.'

'But I'm in my thirties. Time's ticking by. I'd had my chance. I needed to be responsible. There were more people to consider than only me.'

Pia rankled, irritated at being patronised. 'I don't think I'll ever want money that much. Not even when I'm in my forties.'

Cate looked at her, an expression of regret in her face. 'Pia, you walk around in a bubble. It's a lovely bubble, but it's not reality. Yes, you showed me a perfect night but it still cost money and when it came to your own wish-fulfillment a night at the Savoy doesn't come cheap.'

Pia winced at the unguarded reference to their evening.

'Sorry.' Cate pulled back, 'I didn't mean that to come out quite so harshly. I'm sorry.'

Pia flushed in anger and embarrassment. *Is that why you married him? Money?* Pia wanted to say. But she had already overstepped the mark. It was none of her business asking this woman, who was so far beyond her, anything more personal.

Pia stared out at the beginnings of Brixton and the familiar streets. She noticed how dirty they seemed today, despite the renovations from creeping gentrification. Rubbish, old vegetables, fast-food wrappers, all lined the streets from the day's market trade. When they drew into Pia's street, the boarded-up houses stood out. The covered car in her neighbours' front garden, which over the years had lost its wheels and any other parts of value, jarred as she surveyed the street through Cate's eyes.

She turned to her own house and caught sight of Spencer practising his violin next door. It made her smile and her heart swelled with pride for her neighbourhood. The taxi pulled up outside her front door and she snatched up her camera bag.

'Good bye,' Pia said, and she stropped away from the car without glancing back. It might not be the most expensive borough, but she loved it and no amount of money would entice her to move. She wasn't going to feel ashamed of it because of Cate.

A few moments later, she returned more meekly to the taxi.

'Um.' Pia couldn't look Cate in the eye. 'I don't have any cash. Would you mind paying the taxi driver?'

'Of course.'

'I'll pay you back,' Pia mumbled. She sloped around and entered the house with rather less indignation and even less dignity. She shut the front door behind her and leaned back. 'Bollocks.'

Her mother was in the sitting room and peeked over a copy of *El Pais*. She surveyed Pia from head to toe and back again, taking in the plastic-ring and silver-foil look.

'Don't ask,' Pia shook her head. 'Just don't ask.' She ran up the stairs, threw herself on the bed and buried her face in the pillow.

13

Fleet Street was baking in the sun, even at eight in the morning when Pia chained her scooter to a bike rack. Her hair was slick with sweat as she slipped off her helmet. She wasn't the only one suffering from the heat wave, also known simply as summer in other countries. Financiers with their obligatory uniform of suit, striped shirt and red tie, drooped along the street with dark patches of sweat beneath their armpits. Red-faced barristers under black gowns and woollen wigs verged on the edge of explosion or expiry. If there was one thing the British did well, it wasn't any weather that deviated from moderate, not even Brits with Latin blood like Pia.

The offices of *Bennet* on the top floor were stifling. The windows were open but the air was stagnant. Denise on reception held the collar of her top with both hands and wafted it back and forth. Her breasts jiggled so that they reminded Pia of blancmange, sweaty blancmange.

'Wish they'd put bloody air-conditioning in,' Denise said. 'Did you know that it's illegal to work below sixteen degrees? But no bugger thought England would ever get too hot. Stupid bastards.'

Pia wiped her brow. It didn't auger well that even Denise was tetchy this morning. Pia wandered up the corridor to a hot-desk office. Rafe's door was open, his key still in the lock. It was his open-door policy to welcome anyone at any time. But his raised voice from inside wasn't welcoming today.

'Well, where was she last night?' Pia heard him shout.

'Keep a lid on it Rafe,' a confident female voice ordered. 'You're overreacting.'

The heated exchange stopped Pia in her tracks as she passed his doorway. She twitched towards the raised voices. A woman, perhaps in her thirties, held her hand around Rafe's arm. They stood with their backs to Pia, but she could see the woman's face in profile. The familial likeness was obvious, Rafe's handsome looks softened to a female version.

Rafe ran his hand through his hair with agitated fingers. 'She's acting more distant. There's something up.'

'She seemed fine to me,' the woman replied. 'She was running a bit late. She admitted she'd had a crappy day at work, but then we had dinner and I didn't think anything of it.'

'Was she with you all night?' Rafe snapped.

'No. She's a big girl. She went to the loo by herself and I didn't escort her home. I'm not going to report on her every move. You have to trust her.'

Rafe shifted his weight from foot to foot, distressed. Pia could see his whole body wound with tension, his usual positive energy channelled into rage. He snatched his arm away from the woman and swung round.

'For fuck's sake!' His face was red with frustration. He twisted from side to side, his arms flailing. He seemed to be searching for something to vent his anger upon and he halted when he spotted the metal waste paper bin. With angry energy he lashed out and kicked it unrestrained across the office. The bin crashed into the wall and clattered as it bounced away across the floor. The fury in his voice had troubled Pia enough, but seeing his buoyant vitality turn into such rage made her flinch away from the doorway. She shuffled back.

'If I ever get my hands on the fucker...' he shouted.

110

She backed away quicker, scuffing her heels on the carpet as she sped up along the corridor.

'Hey, hey, careful.' A soft conciliatory voice came from behind her. Warm arms enveloped her to cushion the collision. She twirled around knowing without a doubt who was behind her.

'Hi,' Cate said.

'Morning.' Pia sulked and talked down to her feet.

'I'm sorry about yesterday.'

Pia continued to stare at her shoes. She realised that her bottom lip was protruding. She pursed her lips with resolve and peered up, determined to behave like a grown up.

Cate looked tired. Her eyes were dark and heavy as if from a long and troubled night. Was it Cate that Rafe had been angry with? Pia stared into her eyes. Whatever Rafe saw, Pia couldn't see any duplicity there.

'Are you OK?' Cate breathed.

Pia nodded and tried to assume an unaffected appearance.

'It's a good job I bumped into you. I needed to warn you—'

'Benitez-Smith! Gillespie!' This time it was Ed's voice that bellowed. 'My office. Now!'

Cate raised her eyebrows and sucked air through her teeth. 'Too late.'

Pia cowered and followed Cate to Ed's lair. They sat in front of the desk and waited for Ed who stared out the window with fists on her hips. She swirled round.

'Rumour has it,' Ed shouted, 'that at yesterday's show, Elana Devanka was off her tits.'

A bolt of fear shot through Pia.

'Rumour has it that she completely lost it, cried like a baby and wailed for a rat.'

Pia gripped her knees in an effort to keep them from shaking but the tension set off tremors through her whole body.

'Rumour has it that she looked like a stick-thin raccoon that had been shat on by a vulture and mauled by a bear.' Ed flicked her glare between them, her eyeballs protruding. 'Now that sounds like a perfect news item for this shitty little mag. Don't you think?'

Pia blushed and started to open her mouth.

'And,' Ed cut her off with her loudest shout yet, 'rumour also has it that Elana Devanka was spirited away by a kind-hearted reporter and her friend from outer space.'

Pia found herself curling up and studying her hands in a way she hadn't done since school. Out of the corner of her eye she could see Cate, serious but meeting Ed's stare.

'You two need to have a damned good article on my desk by close of business. Otherwise, I don't care who you are or who you've fucked, your arses will be kicked off this magazine. Do I make myself clear?'

They both nodded in silence.

'You've been about as fucking useful as a tampon for an eighty-year-old. Now piss off out of my sight.' And Ed turned her back to them.

They wandered up the corridor. Whether Cate wiped her forehead out of stress or because of the heat Pia couldn't tell. Pia was shaking, from eavesdropping on the angry Rafe and from Ed's tirade. She breathed out trying to calm her nerves.

'I'm sorry. This is my fault,' Pia said.

Cate shook her head. 'No it's not. You didn't need to persuade me. I didn't have the heart to take advantage and ruin a model's career either.'

'Pity it's sunk ours,' Pia added. Her belly felt hollow from the blasts of ill temper she'd witnessed and at the thought of losing her job.

Cate shook her head irritated. 'I can't think in this heat.' She wiped her brow again. 'I thought the after-show party would be the best source of gossip, so I have no material for an article. I hadn't started taking notes. Stupid. I was so stupid.'

'But you were talking to everyone.'

'Empty chit chat. Nothing of substance at all. Apart from the odd good friend.' Cate breathed out long and hard. 'How about you? What did you get?'

Pia coloured. 'I haven't checked yet. I wasn't in the best mood last night.'

A flicker of discomfort twitched across Cate's face. 'I am sorry. I'm—'

At that moment another bout of ill-tempered conversation burst out of Ed's office.

'Come on,' said Cate. 'I've got other jobs I can fall back on. But I don't think you have. How about we go through your photos and see if we can salvage something between us.'

Pia smiled, despite herself. 'Shall we go somewhere a bit calmer and cooler?'

Cate nodded, stress still pinching her features.

Pia took them the length of Fleet Street, past the immoveable block and dome of St Paul's and the financial centre of the city that baked in the morning heat. She stopped at Leon for two takeaway drinks of fresh lemon, mint and ginger and guided a perplexed Cate through the patchwork of old institutions and new office blocks.

'Wait, you'll see.' Pia grinned.

They cut down a small unpromising road past a large bank and at the last moment they saw it: a small old church, St Dunstan's in the East, nestled in between the office blocks. The building hadn't been as lucky as St Paul's in the Blitz and although the tower remained intact it was an empty shell with no roof or interior.

Pia led Cate through the black gates. They ducked in through the gap left by the burned church doors, the remaining archway now overgrown with Virginia creeper. Inside had been landscaped and planted into a serene garden. Cobbled pathways swept around the edges underneath hanging trees that shaded and cooled. A fountain trickled in the old nave of the ruin and the shell walls were wrapped in vines and wisteria. Spaces where stained glass windows had once shone multicoloured beams into the church were now a luminous green of sun-lit foliage.

They sat on the cool shaded grass by the walls and Cate gazed around. 'It's so quiet.'

The only other visitor was a man in a suit, taking a nap on a bench. It was difficult to believe they were in the middle of a world-class financial district.

Pia smiled. 'It gets busier at lunchtime, when people bring their sandwiches, but it's always quiet and calming. People unwind here.'

Pia could see Cate's tension dissipate. She sipped her tangy lemon-mint drink and took in the peaceful atmosphere, her shoulders relaxing.

'Trust you to know of somewhere secret and beautiful like this,' Cate said.

Pia felt the warmth of the compliment and couldn't help but be buoyed by it.

'You can hear birds.' Cate peered over to the fountain where two small sparrows with big attitudes were fighting about something important in the water. She sighed. 'Oh this makes me want to move to the country.'

Pia nodded, feeling the same ache when presented with a small tempting morsel like this. 'I know what you mean.'

'Do you?' Cate sounded surprised. 'I took you for a consummate Londoner.'

Pia shrugged. I love it and I can't think of many places more fascinating. There's always something new or old and exciting round every corner. But I love the countryside too. My dad made sure of that.' She laughed. 'He used to take me walking in the South Downs when I was little, and when I was a baby too. There are pictures of me as a large toddler in a homemade carrier on his back. He cut leg holes in his old army rucksack and lobbed me in.'

She beamed at Cate, elated by the memories.

'You're very fond of your dad aren't you?' Cate said, her head tilted to the side. 'Do you miss him?'

'Yes I do.' Pia didn't hide any of her melancholy. 'He's four years into his sentence, and it's been very hard on mum. But even from inside a prison he's still the best dad in the world.'

Cate smiled at her and looked away. 'I never knew my father. I'm quite envious.'

Pia felt a twinge of sadness and also surprise that Cate found anything of her to envy. She yearned to ask Cate more about her family, past, anything and everything, but Cate's gaze was removed and didn't invite polite enquiry.

'Come on,' Cate said. 'Let's look at those photos.'

They were three pictures into the collection on her laptop when Pia remembered what a large proportion of them featured Cate. There was the empty catwalk with the design team administering last minute changes, with Cate in the foreground waving. Another of the arena filling before the show, crowds filing down aisles, with Cate beautiful in profile. Cate tapped through the pictures while a hot blush crept up Pia's neck. She began to sweat. Cool droplets formed on her back and she swiped at her brow trying to hide her discomfort.

Cate didn't seem to notice and Pia prayed that the later pictures had more variety. Pia sighed with relief at the pictures of excited anonymous guests filling the arena and then groaned when the sequence changed to a close-up of the renowned actress with Cate glowing by her side. Pia covered her eyes when the next photo showed Cate: a beautiful shot that caught her unguarded smile, and also her unguarded cleavage. Cate politely skipped over the image.

'Oh, this is a very good one of her.'

Pia slid her finger to the side and peeped out. It was another close up of the actress. Her face was creased in mirth with, of course, Cate by her side wonderfully exposed.

'If we crop it,' Cate added, so deadpan that Pia blushed to her roots.

Pia closed her eyes and decided that listening to Cate flicking through the photos was torture enough. The laptop clicked for hundreds of photos, as tortuous as a dripping tap, all the while without comment from Cate. Then it stopped. All Pia could hear was the faintest breeze through the leaves above, argumentative sparrows and the hum of the city.

'This is stunning,' Cate whispered.

Pia slipped her hands away, hoping she hadn't taken a shot that had zoomed all the way into Cate's bra.

It was the photo she'd taken by instinct from the hip on the wide-angle lens. Aimed up at the ceiling, it showed the full-bodied models towering above the cat walk. They struck up into the bright, exploding stage lights like heroic statues and, around the edge, were silhouettes of the audience on their feet applauding and worshipping them.

Cate regarded her. 'You've got good shots all the way through, but this one's incredible.'

Pia felt sheepish at the praise. 'It was a lucky shot. I took it without thinking.'

'Rubbish. When I take a photo without thinking I get a blurred shot of my nostrils. This is an excellent shot, and if Ed doesn't keep you on because of this she's insane.'

'Well, she is mad.' Pia sighed.

Cate laughed. 'Indeed. But you know what I mean.' She stared back at the screen. 'I think we can pull an article out of these. The triumph and adoration of nature's wonderful variety—real models take the fashion show by storm. What do you think?'

Pia nodded and grinned.

She wandered the gardens while Cate sat cross-legged on the grass tapping the laptop. She looked younger sitting there, her shoes discarded on the grass and her bare feet tucked beneath her knees. Pia imagined that's how she must have been as a student, studying in the gardens of Cambridge; a beautiful young woman in a simple summer dress with nothing as troublesome as a billionaire husband to complicate her life. A twinge of sadness pulled at her heart and Pia wished she could have met Cate back then.

Cate beckoned Pia over, eager to present her article. 'Could you have a quick read? We're running out of time.'

Pia sat down. She loved Cate's turn of phrase, and the way she appealed to popular tastes while giving the article substance with her articulate insights. Pia felt embarrassed that Cate had asked her to comment on it, it was so beyond her skills.

'What do you think?' Cate asked, wringing her hands with impatience.

'I think you're a very good writer.' Pia was now in awe of Cate more than ever before.

'Do you think Ed will go for it?'

'I don't know. All I know is that I wish I could write like that.'

Cate hesitated. 'That's a lovely thing to say Pia.'

'It's true. I wouldn't lie to you.'

'Always honest,' Cate said, a sad smile on her face. Her hand twitched, and for a moment, Pia thought she might lift her fingers to Pia's cheek. They gazed at each other and Pia was lost in the face she'd first been entranced by in Kensington Gardens. The large eyes, the cheeks flushed rose, those soft full lips. The impulse to lean forward and kiss her was overpowering. She knew how she would taste, how her lips would feel slipping over hers.

Cate blinked, collecting herself, and pulled away. She gulped to clear her throat. 'I'll email it to Ed. With the photos.' And she turned away.

—

When they returned to the office, they peeped round Ed's door. Ed lifted a hand to silence them and continued to stare at her laptop. She was still wearing a frown when she leaned back in her chair.

'Well ladies.' Ed peered over her glasses. 'You've earned yourselves a reprieve. Come and sit down.'

Pia grinned and Cate squeezed her knee as they sat down.

'It's not the scandalous article I was after, but an uplifting read is a good balance for all the other muck we're putting in the first edition. Cate, this is the kind of thing I imagine you could write in your sleep, but Pia.' Ed turned her severe gaze to her and for a moment she thought her reprieve was very short-lasting indeed. 'That photo is magnificent. I've seen all the agency shots from yesterday and there's nothing that touches it. Keep it up shortarse.'

Pia's fright evaporated into elation and she beamed at Cate who gave her a warm smile in return.

'Now,' said Ed. 'There's something I want to try to test out the demographics. It'll be interesting to see how many hits this gets with the online version. I have a very dear and old friend with an interesting story.' She hesitated and glanced at Pia. 'A chat with Cate is all that's strictly necessary, but I have a feeling she'll take a shine to shortarse here and be more forthcoming.'

'Who is she?' Cate asked.

'That you'll find out.' Ed smirked.

Cate raised an eyebrow at Ed's game. 'Do we have to guess where she lives as well?'

Ed hacked up a laugh. 'Ah, she's a cunning old thing. As well a decent bit of cash she wants a nice simple brasserie lunch. By which she means a meal at the Savoy. So you'll meet her there for lunch.'

Cate's face changed in an instant. Her willing engagement in Ed's game switched to mortification and the warmth vanished from the room.

'Is there a problem with that?' Ed said, detecting the change in atmosphere.

When Cate didn't answer, Pia stuttered. 'No, that's great.' She said it with not a milligram of enthusiasm.

'Good. Enjoy it.' Ed frowned. 'And don't get used to working lunches like this. I want you back on soggy sandwiches before you can say cheap marg on white sliced. Now don't fuck up.' Ed ushered them out.

Pia could feel Cate's tension as they walked from the room. As soon as they were beyond ear-shot Pia turned to her.

'I'll see you there.' Cate was brusque and cut her off. She disappeared down the corridor, without another look or word, and Pia stared after her.

14

Pia sat in the garden beneath the artichoke and fennel plants. It was early morning but the sun had already burned off the dew. She could hear the district waking up, the crash of crates of bottles delivered to local stores, the rattle of metal shutters being rolled up from shop windows.

Pia stared at the mug of black coffee in her hands, watching the steam curl around the surface and dissipate in the warm air.

'What you doing out here, mija?' Her mother's face appeared between two artichoke heads.

'Hi Mama,' Pia said, forlorn.

'Oh dear.' Her mother put on an exaggerated grieved expression. 'It cannot be that bad.' She ducked under the vegetation and squeezed her sizeable bottom beside Pia. 'Come on. Tell your mama.'

'Oh there's nothing to tell.'

'Puh.' Her mother looked both unimpressed and unconvinced. 'It's this naughty chica, isn't it?'

Pia sighed. The thought of lying to her mother made a fleeting appearance, but went whizzing by. She nodded.

'What's happened? Has she been bad to my Pia?'

'No. No she hasn't. In fact I don't understand how she's been treating me. That's the problem.' She peered at her mother. 'One minute she's my greatest ally, standing up for me in front of Ed, and the next she freezes on me.'

Her mother frowned. 'How much time do you spend with this Cate, mija?'

'Oh, not loads.' She gave her mother a meek look. 'I've been paired up with her for some assignments.'

'Mmmhuh?'

'She's a brilliant writer and journalist. It's very flattering that I've been assigned to her.'

'And meanwhile she toys with you. Builds you up one moment and leaves you to fall the next.'

'No. It's not like that. She's not a cruel person.' Pia was desperate for her mother to understand Cate. 'She... I... Just... I don't know. Sometimes I think she likes me, as a friend, I mean someone good to work with, and then other times...'

Her mother put her big soft arm around her shoulder and squeezed her into her bosom. 'You are such a romantic fool.'

'No I'm not Mama. I'm not expecting her to change her mind or anything stupid like that.'

'No, true. But you play the jilted lover like a Hollywood movie star.'

Pia deflated.

'First you think you have this love at first sight with this woman.' Her mother threw up her hands. 'Then she scorns you for someone and you are the wronged woman still holding a flame.'

'A candle,'

'Whatever.'

'I'm not stupid enough to think she'd ever want to be with me,' Pia muttered. 'But it's hard seeing her every day. Sometimes I see glimpses of her, how she was that night. She is a nice person Mama.'

Her mother squeezed her tight. 'I know mija. Please try to move on though. Don't mistake this woman being professional and friendly for anything else.'

—

Pia pushed round the revolving doors into the great hall reception of the Savoy and took a tentative step inside. It seemed a different place today. Daylight was harsh and the shoes of guests clipped across the marble floors. She scanned around the sofas trying to find Cate but they were only filled with guests arriving or getting ready for departure.

'She's in Kasper's,' a deep voice said behind her.

The familiar doorman stood to attention with his hands behind his back, not a muscle moving, not even a twitch of his moustache. He peeped at her out of the corner of his eye and winked.

'Thank you.' And Pia shuffled off unnerved in search of Kasper's Seafood Bar and Grill.

The Art Deco style restaurant shone from every corner. Twisting chandeliers graced the ceilings and Pia was almost afraid to step on the dark marble floor that reflected her rather less polished self. Turquoise leather club chairs around low tables seated a mixed clientele from older couples dressed to the nines to young tourists in awe of their surroundings. In the middle of the room was an elegant oval bar with shards of glass lighting hanging from above. She spotted Cate, refined in a simple slim-fitting linen dress, reaching out a hand to greet an elderly lady sat at the bar.

Cate glanced up as Pia approached, her expression difficult to read. Her companion turned around, following her gaze. The woman was dressed in riding boots, a silk shirt and what Cate had described as slacks. She also wore a gleeful smile of recognition on her face.

It took a moment or two for Pia to recognise the erotica reader from the Tube. 'Oh my God.' Pia was unreserved with surprise. 'It's *Spank My Mistress.*'

Pia blushed as several people in the restaurant exclaimed their displeasure and Cate turned away. The woman, however, laughed, threw back her head and clapped her hands together. 'What a wonderful surprise, and such an unusual greeting.' The woman bear-hugged her. 'Ed is a clever woman. What a treat to have you two for lunch.' And she clasped Pia's hand with her bony fingers and led her to sit down.

'You must call me Lottie. "Spank My Mistress" is such a mouthful.' She grinned. 'Although simply "mistress" does sound fine, don't you think?'

Pia sniggered.

'Should we sit down and make a start.' Cate frowned and took a notebook from her bag.

'Oh pish. Plenty of time for work.' Lottie swiped at her hands. 'Let's have a bloody good lunch first.'

They tucked themselves away on a corner bench seat. Lottie sat in the middle, her hands spread across the polished dark-wood table, snug between Pia and Cate.

'Isn't this splendid.' Lottie sighed.

For Pia some of the shine was taken away by the familiar view from the window. The river-side restaurant had the same vista she'd cherished from the hotel room. She blushed at the memory, ashamed of how she'd felt about Cate at the time. The warmth she thought they'd shared contrasted so much with Cate's indifference now.

Cate sat with her back to the window and busied herself with the menu.

'Would you like something from the seafood bar to start?' Cate asked. 'I don't think Ed would mind if we stretched to a small amount of caviar.'

Lottie chuckled. 'That's more the spirit. Oh, speaking of spirit, where's the wine list?' Lottie scanned down the menu and abandoned it with a flick of the wrist. 'Oh, I'll have their Sancerre. I don't have expensive taste.'

Pia glimpsed the price of the wine and kept her amusement to herself. Several meals could be bought for the same price as that vintage.

'What about an oyster as an entrée?' Cate suggested.

'Oh dear no.' Lottie wrinkled her nose. 'You know, I heard a top seafood chef describe them once as "a quintessential mouthful of the sea". Well my dear, I had a mouthful of the sea at Brighton once. This was in the days before anyone worried about sewage. And I didn't like it one bit. I'll go for the old sturgeon ova.'

Cate nodded. A smile couldn't be further from her lips. Pia was torn between laughing with Lottie and wanting to hide under the table to avoid Cate's frostiness.

'Do you know,' Lottie said, 'I fancy the seafood platter. Would you gals like to order one with me? They're such a frightful faff to cook at home.'

Pia grinned and nodded eager to fill her growling tummy. Cate folded away her menu with acquiescence.

—

'Now.' Lottie reached out to hold their hands on each side. 'You must tell me all about it.'

'About what?' Pia said.

'How you finally got together. Was it that night I saw you on the Tube?'

'Oh.' Pia blushed. Cate had twitched her hand clean away off the table. 'No. No. We're not together.'

'Is that so?' Lottie sat back.

She opened her mouth for further enquiry but the arrival of the waiter with the seafood platter interrupted her. Pia breathed out with relief and paid great attention to the food, fearing what Cate's expression might be.

The shining oval dish presented all shapes and sizes of lobster, crab, mussels, some shells Pia guessed might have been clams and then other creatures that she had to group under the heading of a-bit-like-a-snails but she hoped weren't. It was accompanied by a set of cutlery that would make a gynaecologist envious.

The waiter distributed a nutcracker, skewer and other implements of torture, which clinked together in front of Pia. He served a sample of each species and left with no hint as to how to defend oneself with the weaponry provided.

'Gosh. What a spread,' Lottie enthused. Delight shone on her face and she brandished her cutlery with zeal.

With a simple flick of a knife, Cate extracted the cooked insides from a crustacean that Pia couldn't further identify. She squeezed on a drop of lemon juice and ate it with a dainty fork.

Pia stared at her plate with terror. What on earth was the etiquette for eating such a dish? She picked what she recognised as a fish knife and tried to serve herself a prawn that, although cooked, still managed to evade capture.

'So why the devil are you two not an item?' Lottie took a sip of her wine and regarded Cate and Pia. 'I don't think I've ever seen a more suited couple.'

Pia blushed at the return of the conversation to their non-existent relationship. Cate frowned into her lunch and Pia was left to stutter 'No, Cate's nothing, not anything, really nothing like me. Rich. Talented. Elegant.' Pia struggled. 'And married,' she said relieved to find the words that would end Lottie's interest. 'She's very, very married.'

'Well are you my dear?' Lottie said surprised. Cate nodded in solemn response and Lottie raised her eyebrows with puzzlement.

They all turned to their plates: Lottie with gusto, Cate with cool finesse and Pia with trepidation. She took a fork and something like her mother's crochet needle and prodded at her food.

'But you found you liked each other so much that you decided to work together?'

Pia jumped at Lottie's return to the awkward subject matter. Still Cate did not respond.

'Erm no.' Pia shuffled. 'We both started new jobs, which happened to be for the same magazine.'

'Hmm. What a coincidence.'

Pia managed to mumble some kind of agreement and continued to push shellfish around her plate.

'If that isn't the universe trying to tell you something, I don't know what is.' Lottie said it to no-one in particular, and Pia couldn't bear to see Cate's reaction.

'You do realise we're here to interview you?'

Pia looked up, shocked to hear Cate speak. She was even more surprised to see the beginnings of a smile on her lips.

Lottie dropped her cutlery with a crash and burst out laughing. 'Indeed. You must forgive an old lady's obstinacy. The trouble is, the older you get the less time and patience you have. So when you see a couple so right for each other you think why the Dickens don't they just get on with it?'

Cate nodded in acknowledgement and returned to her lunch while Pia squirmed next to Lottie.

Pia tried to whisper, 'She's really beyond me. Please don't go on—'

'Oh don't be so silly.' Lottie cut her off with a rasping breath. 'You're not so dissimilar at all, and the bits that are different are the spice.'

Lottie gave her a wide, knowing smile. 'Now eat up.' She picked up a lobster from the platter and tore off a claw for Pia. 'Your soul mate is getting twitchy to start work.'

Pia grinned and was grateful to accept a piece of food she could eat with her hands and something as familiar as a fork.

—

'Well my dears.' Lottie made herself comfortable in a corner sofa of the Thames foyer. 'I suppose we should get down to business.'

The low-lit room was almost empty except for a gentleman who read the *Financial Times* and two more who played chess. Pia searched for the best backdrop for Lottie's portrait. The centre of the room was dominated by an ornate gazebo. Its iron frame housed a grand piano and Pia trotted over to check the lighting.

'I don't know if your readers will be that interested,' she heard Lottie continue, 'but do you recall an actress Diana Waters? Long before your time of course.'

'Yes I do,' Cate replied. 'She won an Oscar for *The Wild Horses* in the sixties didn't she?'

'Yes, and about time. Of course, she'd done fabulous work up until then: *film noir* and screwball comedies, all overlooked by the Academy.'

Cate breathed out a laugh. 'I loved her in *Huntress of the Night*. She was exquisite and menacing.'

Pia was unable to keep her interest to herself. 'Oh I know her.' She sat down and leaned towards Lottie. 'She's one of my favourite black and white film actresses.'

'Is she?' Lottie raised a mischievous eyebrow. 'I'm sure she would have loved you.'

'Yes, there's something about her in *Huntress of the Night*.' Pia paused in thought. 'That look she has. You can't take your eyes off her. I don't know what it is.'

'My dear.' Lottie patted her knee. 'That will be your gaydar going blip blip blip.'

'No,' Pia said wide-eyed. She peeked at Cate for confirmation but Cate looked stunned. 'The blonde bombshell? She was a lesbian?'

'Indeed.' Lottie smirked. 'She was a lesbian, but she wasn't a natural blonde, and I should know.'

Pia took a moment to understand what Lottie had insinuated, and when the penny dropped her eyes grew wider still.

'No!? No way.'

Lottie nodded. 'I was her bit of fluff. Her bit on the side. For fifty years.'

It took a good few moments for both Cate and Pia to first close their mouths, second regain any capacity for thought before, third, either could speak.

Cate was the first to recover. 'Wasn't she married to Ronald Harris?'

'Yes. He was her first love. They married young when she was still scared of the feelings she had for women.'

'But they remained married until she died?' Cate stuttered.

Lottie was amused at their reaction. 'Their official residence was in Notting Hill. But when Di wasn't working, she lived with me.'

'Did he know?' asked Pia. She struggled to conceive of how everyone could be happy in such an arrangement.

'Of course. Difficult not to over fifty years. The pretty boy wasn't the sharpest pencil in the box, but even he would have spotted that.'

'But was he happy with it?' Pia wondered at having to share a woman he must have loved for so long. 'Why didn't she leave?'

'Oh dear.' Lottie cupped Pia's face in her hands. 'I see this is troubling you.' She leaned back in her chair and gazed at the ceiling in thought. 'It was beneficial to all parties that they stay married. Ron loved her. He loved to be seen and photographed with her. It did his film career no end of good. Di got her beard and to keep her career and I was a kept woman. A very happy lady of leisure.'

'Money,' Pia whispered, disappointed.

She saw Cate twitch. Pia couldn't see her face but Cate sat rigid, her entwined fingers white on her lap.

'Money?' Lottie said. 'Yes, in a way. You have to remember this was a very different era. Homosexuality was illegal, and although it didn't include lesbians we weren't popular.'

'I know,' Pia added. 'But I would have found it difficult to live a lie like that.'

Lottie smiled indulgently at her. 'You live in a time of unprecedented rights and freedom. You have the ideals of the young and free. It's easy to be noble when you can't be thrown in prison for unzipping your trousers with the wrong sex in the bushes of Hampstead Heath.'

Pia frowned, 'But I have those privileges because some didn't hide and were honest and noble.'

'True.' Lottie was serious for a moment. 'I had the privilege of wealth, and it wasn't one I wanted to give up.'

The tension from Cate was palpable, which made Pia's irritation worse. She stood up, feeling awkward. 'I'm sorry. It's hit a nerve. It's none of my business.' Pia couldn't raise a smile. 'I'll let you get on with your interview.' And she stumbled away from the table.

Pia wandered around the room attempting to walk off her frustration under the pretence of testing for portraits. She was annoyed at herself for upsetting Lottie and she was annoyed with Cate. She didn't know when she would stop being annoyed with Cate.

The interview seemed to be going well at least. Cate and Lottie sat together in conspiracy. The range of emotions that quivered across Lottie's face was extraordinary: joy, pride, anger, fear even. Pia began to shoot even though the light was poor. She flicked through the camera screen and the images were coarse in the low light. But it suited Lottie's story.

An idea flickered in her brain and, with a feeling of romantic justice, she took out her old camera. It contained her last ever roll of Neopan black and white film.

It was thrilling to take a few precious pictures without the ability to reel off a hundred and check the results in an instant. She watched Cate and Lottie through the lens, not daring to blink in case she missed that moment. And then she saw it.

Cate leaned forward and pulled Lottie into an embrace. Cate's face was out of view but Lottie looked skywards. Her eyes glistened with tears and her expression hovered on a knife edge between despair and elation.

Pia pressed the shutter and pulled the camera away, filled with cold, nervous energy and praying the old film didn't let her down.

She fumbled backup shots on her digital camera, but she knew she hadn't captured such a moment with that.

—

Cate and Lottie stood together and Pia joined them, a little sheepish.

'Good bye my dears.' Lottie smiled with a tear in her eye. 'The interview has moved me more than I thought it would and it has stirred old waters.'

'I'm sorry,' Pia said. 'I was rude.'

'Don't be silly. It's made me think, and although that's not something I'm overly fond of, it is necessary sometimes.' Lottie sniffed. 'But I am tired now. Until next time. I'm in no doubt that I shall see you two together one day.' And she waved over her shoulder.

They both watched until she had left the room and was no longer in sight. Pia remained staring after her, dreading what Cate would say. She knew she was watching her. Pia wondered if Cate would berate her for ruining the interview or for being just plain rude. She wondered how much Cate cringed at bringing such an uncouth person to this hotel for a one night stand.

She edged round to brave Cate's scrutiny. What she found surprised her. Cate flicked her gaze between Pia's eyes as if afraid of what she thought.

'I'd like to show you something. It might explain things to you. I doubt it'll change your opinion of me, but I would like to try all the same.'

Pia was astounded and stared.

Cate reached out and held her hand. 'Please?'

15

They took the Tube to Holland Park and headed on foot in the direction of Ladbroke Grove.

'This is the way I walked home from school,' Cate said.

As they headed further north, the slick veneer of Kensington borough began to peel away. Cars changed from Jaguars in private parking to Minis on the street. All the while, along every street they walked, there loomed a soaring seventies tower block.

'I went to a private girls' school. I think I must have been the only one to walk home, and certainly the only one in this direction. I can't remember where the other scholarship pupils lived.'

They passed yellow-brick terraces and local shops with rusting vans parked outside until all that was left in front of them was the concrete mass of the block of flats.

'This is where we lived.' Cate peered up at the thirty-one storeys that dominated the skyline. The huge tower was a formidable grey presence even on a summer's day. Its striking service tower stood guard over the rows and rows of boxes for people. With a twinge of reluctance, Pia followed Cate through the dark entrance.

'It's much cleaner and safer than when we lived here,' Cate said, as they stepped into the lift. 'There's quite a premium on the top flats. It wasn't good at all when I was young.' Cate wrinkled her nose as if detecting the bad smell of the past. 'It was built as a mixed tenure building, but it was always unpopular and went downhill very quickly.'

Cate led Pia through a narrow, windowed corridor along the outside of the tower. It was quiet given the number of people that must have been within a stone's throw. The thought was unnerving: not being able to see your neighbours or for them to hear you. It felt lonely.

Cate stopped at a blue door that was long overdue attention and a new coat of paint.

'This was Mum's flat. She lived here from a week after I was born to the day she died. She passed away in her bed. Breast cancer.' Cate faltered.

She searched through her shoulder bag and, to Pia's surprise, took out a key and opened the door.

It was dark and stale inside. The windows were drawn over with thick curtains.

'It's the same as the day she died, save a few of my belongings. I was living at university at the time and had my essentials in Cambridge.'

Cate switched on the light to illuminate a small living room. A large brown sofa filled half the room and faced a television, one like Pia's mother used to have with wooden sides.

'You don't know how many hours she spent on that sofa,' Cate laughed.

She led Pia through to a small kitchen with a couple of old units, a stained sink and an electric cooker with furred and greased-up rings.

'That's where she spent most of her time though.' Cate opened the doors to a balcony where a worn armchair faced the railings.

'Wow,' Pia said when she saw the view. Miles and miles of capillary terraces, swathes of parks, railway line arteries and the heart of the city erupting into the skyline.

'You can see Kent on a clear day, but that's where my mother used to stare.' Cate thrust out her slim arm and elegant fingers in front of her. 'If you look down the line between Hyde and Holland Park, can you see a small green area with trees, beyond some tennis courts?'

Pia squinted along the line of Cate's finger. 'With the large red-brick mansion?'

'That's where my mother grew up and where my grandparents still live.'

Pia stared at Cate's distant ancestral home. Its revelation hadn't been what she expected from the visit to the block of flats.

'Mum was a bit of rebel.' Cate continued. 'She left boarding school at sixteen against my grandfather's wishes.' She nodded towards the mansion. 'When he found her in bed with a woman twice her age he kicked her out.'

'What's wrong with older women?' Pia quipped.

'It was the just the woman part.' Cate smiled. 'Mum was also one of the first Greenham Common women in the early eighties. She was part of the peace camp protesting against nuclear missiles at the RAF base.' Cate's eyes twinkled with pride and amusement. 'When you consider my grandfather comes from a proud family of military officers, that was quite a radical thing to do.'

Pia found so many questions popping into her head, but Cate seemed such a mix of emotions that she held her tongue.

'I imagine if she'd towed the line after that he may have come round with my grandmother's encouragement, but she fell for another woman in the camp. They swore their love for each other. Wanted children together. They came to some agreement. I don't know whether it was one of those drunken conversations, I could never tell from Mum. But they agreed that if either had the chance to sleep with a man they would try to get pregnant and have a family together. My mum did. I think the reality was too much for her partner, and she left. This is where Mum ended up, alone with me.'

Cate turned to Pia, her face heavy with fatigue and her smile flat.

'And your grandparents never forgave her?' Pia was incredulous. 'Never helped?'

'My grandmother did, in secret. They developed this building, among others in London. My grandmother signed up this flat in someone else's name. It was one of the few things she managed to do behind my grandfather's back. He'd disowned my mother entirely and made sure she wouldn't inherit anything from him.'

'But what about you? Didn't he want his granddaughter to grow up somewhere nicer?'

Cate gave a slight shrug. 'My grandfather wouldn't see me until I was a teenager. He didn't acknowledge I existed.'

'But why?' Pia said in disbelief. 'It wasn't your fault, any of the arguments between them.'

Cate glanced up recalling, 'According to my grandfather I was "that bastard girl".'

Pia flinched at the term. It was harsh for any child. 'But you're his flesh and blood, regardless of who your father was.'

Cate's face was stiff with tension. 'I don't think he wanted to acknowledge that my mother was even his.'

Pia was shocked. 'And now? Is he any better since your mother died?'

Cate nodded. 'A little, because of Wynne, my grandmother's, efforts. I'm still the bastard child though.'

'But, but…' Pia was lost for words. 'You hadn't done anything wrong.'

Cate shrugged. 'They were very similar personalities despite their polar opposite lifestyles and politics. When they argued, Wynne said it was like a tornado. My grandmother and I were collateral damage.'

Pia couldn't think of anything consoling to say. She found it hard enough to conceive of anyone doing such a thing. She stared out over the cityscape to the manor, wondering how the sight of it would have eaten away at Cate's mother, a daily reminder of riches from the view of a brutalist concrete tower. And Cate's craving for luxury struck home.

'I never knew my father,' Cate said. 'My mother and grandparents were estranged and then I lost Mum. It made me feel very vulnerable.' Cate didn't meet her eyes, but Pia could see that fragility in her demeanour.

'I dread being left alone,' she continued. 'I fear the loneliness or getting ill without enough money to pay for care. I watched Mum staring out from this balcony for too many years not to have that fear ingrained.'

Pia nodded. She did understand. She could see the fear gripping Cate at that moment. She reached out, wanting to close the gap between them and comfort her, to reassure her that she wasn't alone.

But Cate stiffened and looked away. 'Rafe was always very good to me. We were friends at college and his sister is also a good friend of mine. He was very supportive when Mum died. We made a good pair, I thought. It would have been Mum's birthday today,' Cate added, and they were silent again.

The mention of Rafe numbed Pia, but it was childish to indulge in jealousy in view of Cate's confession. She forced herself to shake it off and tried to think of a lighter subject.

'What were you like?' Pia tilted her head. 'What were you like when you were younger?'

Cate turned towards her smiling. 'Oh, I was a good girl. Swotty. I loved reading and I was always curled up in the corner with a book at home. I did well at school. Of course, you can get away with murder once in a while if you behave the rest of the time.'

'Oh really?' Pia asked, interested.

'I broke into the cricket pavilion at the boys' school when I was fourteen. I wanted some private time with my first girlfriend.' She grinned. 'We didn't mean to break in; the window we forced fell apart. We were all asked to stay behind after assembly. The headmistress was in a thunderous mood after reports of two suspicious girls running away from the boys' grounds.'

'What did you do?'

'Owned up.' Cate shrugged. 'I went to the headmistress' office. I told her I'd gone there with my girlfriend and that it had been an accident. She gave me detention for a week and that was that. Although I remember now.' Cate frowned. 'She advised that I not mention the girlfriend if I confessed to anyone else. You know, come to think of it she must have been a lesbian.'

Pia laughed. 'I bet she had a soft spot for you.'

'Yes, she did; in no dubious way either. She helped me get into Cambridge when no-one else cared. She was very nice.' Cate paused, a keen interest in her eye. 'What about you? What were you like?'

'Me? I was naughty.' Pia giggled. 'Not in a gone wild way. I just wouldn't pay attention to subjects I didn't like. It used to drive Mama crazy. She blamed Dad of course. He used to encourage me at things like art, but he had no heart for maths and sciences.' Pia peeked back at the flat, curious. 'Do you have any photos of you at school?'

Cate thought for a moment and nodded. She ducked back inside and returned with a framed photo: a black and white image of a group of girls on the verge of being women. 'This was in the sixth form.'

'I've spotted you.' Pia grinned. Cate stood in the middle of the front row, a shy but at the same time confident smile on her lips. She was tall and athletic and already had that poise that the other girls lacked and perhaps would never have.

'I bet you were head girl,' Pia said.

138

Cate laughed and nodded.

—

A key in the door startled them. Cate stepped into the flat and Pia lingered, watching through the window. A small elderly lady entered, her eyes cast on the floor, not expecting company. She was smartly dressed in a blue blazer. When she spotted Cate her face rippled with grief.

'Oh darling, I had no idea you still came here.' She reached up towards Cate and kissed her on the cheek.

'I didn't realise you did,' Cate replied.

The woman raised her hand to dismiss her concern. 'Just on her birthday. Charles won't do a thing. He leaves the house and refuses to visit the cemetery. I prefer to come here and sit with her instead. If you understand.'

'Yes of course.' Cate leaned down and held the woman. 'I brought a friend. I should introduce you.'

The two women came out onto the balcony, Cate's arm entwined with the older woman's.

'This is Pia,' Cate said. Pia straightened her shoulders and put out a hand to greet the visitor. 'This is my grandmother, Lady Wynne.'

The old woman clasped Pia's hand as a reflex, but when she met her gaze she was startled. Pia was puzzled for a moment, but then realised that her boyish looks might be controversial.

'I work with Cate,' she stuttered, trying to diffuse any concern that her granddaughter might be following in her daughter's footsteps.

'It's a pleasure to meet you,' Lady Wynne said, appearing to wish no further conversation.

When Cate drew Lady Wynne inside to make herbal tea Pia stayed on the balcony, not wanting to intrude. It was no hardship, spending some time surveying the city she adored. It was like looking at a graphic map from her vantage point.

From time to time she heard their voices, muffled from inside the flat: Lady Wynne retelling Cate stories of her mother in her youth, catching Cate's profile in the light that was so like her mother's.

'I don't know how much longer I can hold on to the flat,' Lady Wynne said. 'Charles is belly aching about refurbishing. He seems to think everyone wants to live in the sky these days. "Look at the Shard," he says.'

'I'm not sure the Tower of Terror can be rebranded to appeal like the Shard,' Cate replied, being politic.

'Tell that to the silly old coot,' Lady Wynne replied. 'He wants to start kicking out the tenants and knock through flats to convert them into luxury apartments.'

Outside, Pia tutted to herself. 'Just what London needs: more bloody luxury flats.'

She stared over the expanse of London below, watching and listening to the traffic, birds and trains. It took a few seconds for her to register the silence from within.

'Well.' Lady Wynne's voice was loud and clear behind her. 'We have a fiery one here.'

Pia spun round. 'I'm sorry. I was just being…rude.' She deflated.

'You were being honest, and it's not an opinion that is foreign to me. So what would you do with it?' Wynne raised an eyebrow.

Pia's irritation was roused again. 'I'd keep it affordable. For people who need to live and work here. People everyone needs like nurses, cleaners, teachers, people in shops. You know, ordinary people. There are an awful lot of them.'

'Indeed,' said Lady Wynne. 'We have to keep the servants somewhere. In the good old days, we used to build quaint little houses for them out the back.'

Pia opened her mouth, shocked at the change in perspective.

Lady Wynne tapped her under the chin. 'I'm joking my dear.'

'Oh.' Pia closed her mouth.

'I think these flats are fine as they are. Some are large enough for families. Greater numbers of small flats don't give us a vastly reduced income in any case. But, it lacks prestige on our property portfolio. That's the problem.' She shrugged and looked at Pia. 'Tell me, where do you live?'

'Brixton.' Pia hesitated. 'With my mum. And when she gets sick of the sight of me I have no idea where I'll be able to afford to live. I'll probably have to commute from Birmingham.'

'Oh my dear.' Lady Wynne reached out in sympathy. 'I do hope it doesn't come to that.'

'I don't think Birmingham's as bad as…You're joking.'

'That's right.'

Pia grinned, seeing a little of Cate in the older woman.

16

Lady Wynne's chauffeur followed Holland Park Avenue and turned up through Notting Hill. The colourful terraces changed to taller mansion flats and the road became leafier and more exclusive. At the top of the hill, the driver stopped at gates to a large green area enclosed by a brick perimeter wall. The gates opened without a sound or visible human assistance and the driver pulled around the generous turning circle in front of the mansion.

It was larger than Pia had thought from a distance. A central buttress of red brick rose above the wide steps and was flanked by two wings. Attic rooms peeped out of the sloping slate roof. Pia felt naïve. She hadn't thought houses like this existed in London, or at least ones that weren't owned by royalty or a charitable trust.

Pia slipped off the leather seat from the back of the car and waited, feeling a little self-conscious, while the driver aided Cate and Lady Wynne.

'It's a beautiful day.' Lady Wynne gazed at the cloudless sky. 'I think we should have lemonade on the east lawn.'

Pia nodded, unwilling and unable to object to anything.

'I'll get Wilkins on it,' Lady Wynne continued. 'Cate, I'd like a quick word with you inside. Pia, please make yourself at home.'

Cate smiled back at Pia before she was whisked up the grand steps and into the house. Pia turned to the gardens and wondered how one should go about making oneself at home in several acres.

She ambled down steps onto a narrow lawn with exuberant long borders on either side. Waves of flowers, golds, reds and whites, rippled in the gentle breeze. The fragrance was uplifting. A hint of honeysuckle washed over her and the powerful smell of jasmine filled her head.

She ducked under a yew archway and the lawn opened out into a broad expanse of grass in perfect stripes. Not a blade seemed out of place and it was unimaginable that a dandelion or daisy might blight the uniform green.

Pia stared at it in disbelief. She laughed and removed her shoes and socks. She meandered around, squeezing her toes into the cool dense grass. The sensation of soft padded lawn beneath the soles of her feet was sensual, and it was a perverse pleasure on such an uptight lawn.

The grass gave way to imperfections where a small wood began. Pia sat down, more relaxed among the clover and cushioning moss with the odd daisy for company. She lay down and peeped through the branches of a beech tree at the sky. The sun winked through the leaves. She closed her eyes, enjoying the intermittent warmth followed by a cooler kiss as the dappled shade flickered across her face.

'This is my favourite part of the garden.' Cate's soothing voice roused her. Pia blinked to and saw her tall silhouette above.

'Don't get up,' she whispered. 'I'll join you.'

Cate curled up beside her, and Pia noticed her feet were also bare. It was difficult not to admire Cate's body. Pia gazed along the exquisite shape of her legs that fell into inviting shadows under her dress. She admired the curve of her hip and fall of her belly. She knew her breasts by heart now, the way they lay in clothes. She couldn't help but linger there, remembering how they felt against her own.

She admired Cate's shoulders, neither weak nor athletic. They were left bare by the dress and a dusting of light freckles invited Pia's mental touch. Pia smiled in a haze, filled with the heady warmth from the sunshine and Cate's scent.

Cate's expression drew her attention. A question seemed to hover on her lips and Pia thought she knew what she wanted to ask.

'I do understand now,' Pia said. 'At least a little.'

Cate gave her a sad smile.

'Although.' Pia frowned. 'I don't understand why you left *The Times*.'

'A favour to Rafe.' Cate sighed and rolled onto her back. 'He wanted some credible journalists to kick off the magazine. I was a natural choice for him.' Cate shrugged. 'The timing was unfortunate though. I had an offer of a twelve-month secondment to the *New York Times*. Delaying the wedding and backing out of the magazine would have been too much to ask. But it is one of the things I regretted immediately.'

'You married a man instead of going to New York,' Pia said with exaggerated consternation. 'I can forgive you everything, but passing up an opportunity to live in New York, crazy.'

Cate laughed. 'Is that somewhere you'd like to visit?'

'It's right there at the top.' Pia shot her arm into the air. 'I would love to live in New York. Not forever, may be a year or two. I'd adore wandering Manhattan, photographing everything from the Brooklyn Bridge to Grand Central Terminal, and people watching in the streets.'

'Me too. For some reason I've always wanted to sit in Central Park and eat a New York pretzel. Since I was little girl. See the Grand Canyon, walk on the moon and eat a New York pretzel: those were my top three wishes when I was seven years old.'

'Were you granted one wish and wished for three more?'

Cate grinned. 'Probably.'

'What else would you do in New York?'

Cate squinted in thought. 'Ice-skating at Rockefeller Centre.'

'Window shopping at Macy's?'

'Meet a stranger on top of the Empire State Building.'

Pia hesitated. 'What would be your perfect day in New York?'

'For under ten pounds?' Cate asked, raising an eyebrow.

'I'll let you spend as much as you want this time.'

Cate was quiet for some time. She was treating it as a more serious question than Pia intended. 'My perfect day? I would have eggs Benedict for breakfast. I would interview someone like Hillary Clinton if she was in town. Then a walk through Central Park over to Café Lalo to type up my piece for the *New York Times*. Then home to a tiny central apartment, to spend the evening in the arms of the person I loved.'

Pia didn't know what to say. It was such a contrast with her idea of a perfect night when they'd first met. She was touched by the change in Cate and emotional at how their dreams dovetailed.

'I don't think I could come up with anything better,' Pia said. 'Except I'd be taking photographs instead of interviewing.'

Cate smiled and rolled onto her side to face Pia. Sunlight streamed through her hair, which flowed loose around her cheeks and caressed her neck. It was if she'd turned to Pia in bed, a tender expression upon her face, and Pia thought how much she would give to wake up to that sight every morning.

'Here you are.' Lady Wynne broke the moment.

Pia sprung up as soon as she spotted Wynne carrying a tray of lemonade. 'Let me.' She grabbed the tray, which rattled with clinking glasses and ice cubes that had escaped the jug.

'We should go and sit somewhere more comfortable,' Cate said. 'We could go to the summerhouse?'

'Nonsense, my dear. I shall be fine. I don't get to roll around in the grass nearly often enough.' Lady Wynne sat down with a bump, which caused Pia and Cate to wince more than she.

Cate's phone buzzed and she excused herself. Lady Wynne waved her hand unconcerned and Cate wandered a little distance away between the trees.

Wynne poured their drinks and handed a glass to Pia. 'You two look quite at home.'

'It's lovely here.' Pia could be nothing but effusive about their hiding place.

'I adored this little bit of wilderness when I was a girl,' Wynne said. 'Charles insists on the bloody lawns being rolled. The man would have a fit if he saw the photos of it as a veg patch during the war.'

Lady Wynne leaned back and gazed towards Cate. 'It's wonderful to have her home. She's not been here anywhere near enough. So much more relaxing when Charles is out too. He's off killing birds on some chum's estate, or something important like that, or more likely killing some chum by accident because he refuses to wear his damned glasses.' She dismissed him with a wave of her hand. 'So much lost time.' Wynne sighed. 'A place like this needs young people.'

'Do you have other grandchildren?' Pia asked, sipping her cool lemonade.

'No. We only had Cate's mother. Shame. I so miss the sound of mischievous feet and naughty laughter around the place. It was filled with visiting cousins during the summer holidays. Best time of my life.'

Pia gulped away a jealous feeling and offered the obvious consolation. 'Perhaps you'll have great grandchildren soon.'

'Perhaps. Perhaps.' Wynne sounded distant. 'I'm not sure Rafe is the fatherly type.' She turned to Pia. 'Tell me, does it bother you that you can't have children?'

For a moment, Pia's brain could have been an empty space where tumbleweed rolled. 'Oh, because I'm a lesbian?'

'Yes.'

'Lesbians can still have children. They don't whip out your ovaries as soon as you come out.'

Lady Wynne burst out laughing. She squeezed Pia's arm. 'Of course not my dear, I meant that you can't make a child together.'

'I don't know. I'm not sure I've ever thought about it like that.'

'You don't want children?'

'Yes I do. I've just never thought it would be a problem.' She pondered for a few moments. 'If she had a baby, I suppose I would see the child of the woman I adored and fall in love with all those bits I recognised from her, and all the pieces in between.' She met Wynne's gaze. 'I can't imagine not loving a baby that she loved. Does that make sense?'

'Yes it does my dear.' Wynne's lips curled and her smile creased her cheeks.

Pia blushed, alarmed, when she realised she'd imagined having Cate's children. She'd pictured Cate, voluptuous and blooming from pregnancy with a tiny baby nestled on her breasts. Her heart skipped and she hoped Lady Wynne hadn't discerned her thoughts. Desperate, she tried to remember the words she'd used. Wynne's stare was penetrating. It made her want to hide.

Pia stood up flustered and stuttered an excuse. 'Sorry. I need the loo.'

'You'll find one.' Wynne waved in the direction of the mansion. 'There's a dozen, so you'll bump into one sooner or later.'

148

Pia shuffled off towards the house more in discomfort from the conversation than from any need to pee. The large entrance hall, with twin stairs joining in the middle, seemed an unlikely place for a lavatory. She imagined that they hadn't fitted a convenient space-saving downstairs loo in a cupboard. Which was a shame, since there was no sign of one in the library, ballroom, parlour or recreation room.

She skipped upstairs, the discomfort of needing to pee now more urgent than the need to avoid further discourse. Pia expected to find a large family bathroom at the top of the stairs, so an extended gallery of family portraits was another source of disappointment.

The first room she peeked inside appeared to be a master bedroom: an enormous bed with his and hers arrangements of books, brushes, mirrors and suits on either side of the room. The en suite door was ajar and inviting. She could see the bowl from where she stood. But, warm and welcoming though Lady Wynne had been, Pia wasn't sure that it extended to placing her warm behind where gentry sat.

The next room was more like a museum. A four-poster bed with thick tapestry curtains was guarded by shining, empty suits of armour. No en suite, only a chamber pot beneath the bed. Although the thought of using a potty was beginning to have a certain appeal she thought she could hold on.

She ran along the wing, checking from side to side, into dressing rooms, empty bedrooms, an old school room, and she had no further choice than to climb up a wooden twisting staircase to the attic. Sure that this would hold one of the dozen toilets, she began to relax her bladder. She was rewarded with a long single room with not even an old rocking horse to haunt it.

'Bugger,' Pia said, with a high pitch of despair. With illogical desperation she crashed open an attic window and leapt onto the roof. While a potty hadn't been inviting a few minutes earlier, the gutter and flared top of a lead drain pipe on the edge of the external wall was now mecca.

She dropped her trousers, stuck out her bottom and hoped that the whole of London wasn't watching, and that any stray hairs wouldn't make her pee down the wall. She sighed as her bladder deflated.

'Ooooooooh. Thank God for that,' she breathed. She closed her eyes, enjoying the relief.

With a last drip and wiggle she started to pull up her trousers.

'You there!'

She peeped over her shoulder, and beyond the white mounds of her buttocks, to see an elderly gentlemen shouting up from the drive: an elderly gentleman wearing a cap and tweed jacket and holding a shotgun.

Still in a squat position she hoisted up her trousers and scurried back inside the attic. She heaved for breath and her eyes were wide as she tried to think of a reason why she might be baring her bottom to Kensington.

Pia consoled herself that something would occur to her while she shuffled through the attic, back along the corridor and to the hall stairs. Nothing. Not a single good reason. She liked to pride herself on her honesty and integrity, but at that moment she would have loved to have been the biggest, dirtiest liar on the planet.

The gentlemen strode across the hallway, shotgun cocked over his arm, and Pia limped down the stairs with shame and a small, uncomfortable wet patch.

'Well who the bloody hell are you?' he shouted. He proceeded past her and peered up and around the stairs.

Confused, Pia tried to catch his eye. 'I was up on the roof.' She gestured over her shoulder. 'You saw me.' And then she kicked herself.

'That was you?' He came up closer and squinted at her. 'Oh. You look different close up. Could have sworn you had a beard from down there. Wynne's right, I should wear my glasses. Well who the bloody hell are you?'

'Pia,' she stuttered.

The man, whom she assumed to be Sir Charles, appeared unimpressed. 'Hell of a London accent you've got there Peter.'

'Peter?' Pia thought that telling someone they've mispronounced your name was one thing. But saying you're not a boy, you're a lesbian and one who's peed down their drainpipe to a homophobic knight was another. So she decided to say 'Yes,' just an octave lower.

'Surname?' bellowed Sir Charles.

'Benitez-Smith.'

'Well Benitez-Smith. What the hell are you doing in my house?'

'I'm a friend of Cate's, sir, and I was, erm, going to the loo.'

'Oh,' he said, still with disdain. 'You should have used the one under the stairs. Genius idea. Everyone should have one. Is Cate here?'

'Yes sir.' Pia was already getting a sore throat from the forced deep voice.

'Didn't know she had any Spanish friends. I assume you're Spanish.'

'I work with her sir and yes, Mama's from near Gibraltar.'

'Hmm.' He squinted, considering her. 'What do you think of this latest debacle? Damned Spanish intruding on fishing rights. They'll be after the Rock itself next.'

Pia wondered if she might be shot if she said the wrong thing. But pretending to be some chap called Peter was already a significant lie for someone so honest, and she couldn't stretch to another. 'I can see their point of view, sir. Isn't still owning Gibraltar a bit like Spain having sovereignty over Cornwall?'

'Pah! Load of old tin mines and tourists. They're welcome to it. But interesting perspective, Peter.' Sir Charles snapped around and stared out into the gardens. 'I'd better say hello to Catherine. I suppose Wynne's with her.'

'Last I looked.'

'Well good. Come on then.'

Pia squared her shoulders, drew in her breasts and tummy, tucked under her bum and strode forward hoping she didn't strain anything in her attempt to walk like a man.

'I suppose you work with that Rafe as well,' Sir Charles said.

'Yes,' Pia growled.

'You know, he's a very savvy businessman. Looks like a fag, but has the balls for earning money.'

Pia winced at the term and prickled with sweat at the prospect of being revealed as a lesbian.

'He's been a revelation with this fracking idea,' Charles continued. 'Could earn a small fortune from our land in Kent.'

Pia rolled her eyes and wondered, not for the first time, how Cate stomached some of Rafe's credentials.

'Ah, here they are. What the devil's Wynne doing lying on the ground?'

'I'll go and see.' And Pia ran on ahead.

She didn't even have time to explain. Wynne and Cate struggled to their feet, clearly alarmed at the prospect of Sir Charles meeting Cate's lesbian friend. Pia gasped for breath and managed to say, 'Please, just go with it.'

'What on earth are you doing here?' Sir Charles bellowed. 'Whole of the grounds and mansion and you sit under a tree.'

'We're fine darling.' Wynne's expression questioned Pia with alarm. 'Is everything OK?'

'Yes, yes. Fine,' Sir Charles said. 'Shot through the window of an old worker's cottage on Geoffrey's estate.

Terribly angry fellow who lived there quite spoiled the mood of the shoot, so we called it a day. Peter here has been entertaining me with his interesting views on sovereignty.' And he slapped Pia on the back.

Pia would have explained at this point if she'd been able to draw breath. As it was she coughed and wheezed and stared, anxious, at Cate, whose initial look of shock and horror was softening to amusement.

'That's wonderful darling,' Wynne said. 'I'm glad you've taken to Peter. Now.' She took Charles' arm and moved to return to the house. 'Let's put the shotgun away before we go any further.'

Lady Wynne and Sir Charles walked away arm in arm. Cate slipped beside Pia and took her hand. 'Why does he think you're a man?' she whispered, delight curling at the corner of her lips.

'Apart from being almost blind? I don't know, but I was flustered and it seemed like a good idea at the time.'

Cate squeezed her close. 'Trouble finds you, doesn't it Benitez-Smith?' And Pia couldn't help be buoyed by Cate's indulgent smile as they walked arm in arm.

Before she left, Lady Wynne came to say goodbye. Cate conversed with her grandfather while Wynne cozied up to Pia. 'I am sorry the silly fool thinks you're a boy, but it was perhaps for the best.' She sighed. 'Before you leave though, I wanted to invite you to a party we're having for Cate. It's a small birthday party, a hundred guests, but I believe you'll recognise one or two from the magazine and feel at home.'

Pia beamed, relieved she hadn't appalled Lady Wynne.

'Lovely to meet such a special friend of Cate's,' Wynne said. 'You know, I don't think she's ever shown anyone her mother's flat. Not even Rafe.' She squeezed Pia's hands and kissed her on the cheek, and the look Cate gave her as she observed warmed her through and through. It was a mix of trepidation, amusement, fondness and pride and it kept Pia on a thrilling high all the way home to Brixton.

She closed the front door behind her, still grinning from the day. She thought of beautiful, refined Cate, and how Lady Wynne had thought of Pia Benitez-Smith from Brixton as her particular friend. She could feel her cheeks glowing.

She heard the flick of a newspaper from the lounge and saw her mother's quizzical expression mocking her again.

Pia sighed. 'I know. I know. But she's becoming a good friend. I like her very much as a person now I understand her better.'

Her mother appeared unmoved.

'She's just a friend, Mama.'

Her mother flicked her paper straight and Pia heard, 'Tut, tut, tut. If I looked like that after seeing my friends at cards, their husbands would ban card night.'

Pia giggled. 'Night Mama.'

'Night mija.'

17

'Frosty today,' Denise murmured from reception.

'Is it?' Pia was incredulous. She wiped the sweat across her forehead from her ill-advised jog up the baking stairwell.

Denise winked at her, an inept movement that involved her mouth grimacing and showing half her teeth.

'Huh?'

The receptionist nodded her head in the direction of the corridor.

Pia turned to see Rafe and Cate walking away, a good stiff yard apart. They disappeared into an office next door to Ed's without a word.

'Hope the office party's still on,' Denise said through a strand of gum. 'You going?'

'Don't know.' Pia gazed towards where Rafe and Cate had been. Rafe was to host a party that evening to celebrate the first edition of *Bennet*. The entire office had been invited to his luxury apartment. When the invitation was circulated, Pia hadn't been sure if she could stomach the residence of the happy newlyweds, but now she was more than a little curious.

'Go on. It'll be a laugh. That Rafe's a good laugh anyhow. Dunno how he ended up with that wife of his though.'

Pia was also about to express her incomprehension when Ed's stern face appeared, along the corridor and a foot or two above her.

'Pia,' Ed said, her head poking out of her office, 'a word please.'

As always, Pia's stomach leapt at the invitation into Ed's office, a prospect always fraught with potential danger and surprise.

A large print copy of an article lay on Ed's desk. Pia's photo of Lottie and Cate in the Savoy was displayed in the corner. Pia grinned despite herself and picked it up. She'd caught it: Lottie clinging over Cate's consoling shoulder with an expression that shivered between despair and elation. The old black and white film had brought a quality to it, a subtle impression of the past: perfect for an article about an old film star.

Ed was watching her and Pia's unease deepened into worry. 'Is it OK?'

'Pia, it's astonishing.'

'Oh good. It looked perfect through the lens.'

Ed took off her glasses. 'It's remarkable. Pia, you have an incredible talent for portrait photography. You capture very personal moments but in a sympathetic way and the composition is inspired. You must spread your wings and do more challenging work than this terrible rag.'

'I'm finding it pretty challenging so far.' The supermodel kidnap sprang to Pia's mind.

Ed shook her head. 'Cate's piece is brilliant too: entertaining, poignant and well balanced. The pair of you should be doing serious journalism.'

Pia beamed, thrilled to be classed with Cate in Ed's high estimation.

'Has Cate seen the photo by the way?' Ed asked.

'Yes, I showed it to her earlier. She loved it.'

'And she's all right with us using it?'

'Yes?' Pia asked, confused. 'Why?'

Ed frowned. 'Well, the pose is quite sexual in a way.'

'Is it?' Pia tipped the photo from side to side.

'What I mean is that Lottie is embracing her as if she was the love of her life, not simply remembering her.'

'Oh,' Pia said. 'So?'

'So the connotation is that Cate is gay.'

'And?'

'Oh dear God. Stop being so dense shortarse.' Ed puffed out in despair. 'Is that an aspect of her life that she wants put into question? Does Cate want, however subliminally, to be presented as a lesbian?'

Pia was a little piqued. 'And what's wrong with being a lesbian?'

'Oh nothing at all my dear. I've enjoyed it immensely since I kissed my convent school teacher when I was fourteen. But that doesn't mean Cate thinks so.'

Pia stared opened-mouthed at the formidable and tall figure of Ed. 'You're a lesbian?'

'You seriously didn't spot it?'

'Sorry. Faulty gaydar.'

'Shortarse, you are a piss poor excuse for a dyke if you can't spot me as a carpet muncher.'

'Oh,' sighed Pia, deflating. 'People surprise me all the time.'

At that moment, they heard raised voices from the office next door. Pia blushed, recognising Rafe's voice followed by Cate's softer tones. She shuffled and tried to pretend she was studying the photograph again.

'Those two have got to sort things out.' Ed nodded in the direction of the wall.

Pia blushed. 'I hadn't noticed there was anything wrong.'

'Really.' Ed raised an eyebrow. It wasn't a question, or an exclamation of surprise, just plain disbelief. 'For a start, I don't think Cate has ever been committed to this magazine. She was distracted and underwhelmed at the kickoff meeting. If you were tall enough you might have

157

seen. Of course, I suppose there could be other issues?' Ed tilted her head to the side in expectation.

Pia tensed with alarm, but for once was sensible enough to stay silent.

'Well, among other things,' Ed continued, 'Cate turned down a secondment to the NYT. I'm surprised it didn't make her choke coming to this rag instead.'

Pia frowned at her, not for the first time rankled by Ed's dismissal of the magazine. 'Why do you work here? You have no respect for this magazine.'

'Money, darling. This pays twice what the broadsheets gave me as a senior editor.'

'Money,' Pia muttered. 'Why is it always money?'

Ed flicked her hand in a dismissive wave. 'Oh I know at your age it doesn't seem to matter and money isn't very romantic. When I was young I was quite happy pissing, snorting and smoking it away. But this side of fifty, darling, things are a little different. If I'm going to retire and live in the lap of luxury, and preferably in the lap of a young floozy, then I need cash.'

Pia grumbled. 'Young floozy? I didn't think you were the type.'

'You're right, quite right. Old floozy, young floozy. I don't mind. Just so long as it's a floozy.'

Pia broke into a smile. 'I suppose that sometimes there's nothing better than a floozy.'

'Except two floozies.'

'Or three floozies,' Pia laughed.

'Indeed. But three is the absolute maximum, because then you run out of hands and tongue and—'

'Stop.' Pia spread both hands in front of her. 'I do not want to know.'

Ed rolled her eyes. 'Piss poor excuse for a dyke.'

—

The sky was deepening to dark indigo when Ed opened the door of her old Mini. 'Hop in shortarse.'

The small car was roomy enough for someone like Pia, but the six feet of Ed was awkwardly folded over the steering wheel.

'You look like you're driving a toy car.' Pia giggled.

'I know it's quite absurd, but the heart wants what the heart wants.' Ed sighed, and she patted the leather steering wheel.

With a roar from the engine and a fart from the exhaust pipe, the small car scooted down Fleet Street. They headed further into the city and out across the river. The Thames glittered with boats and the illuminated Tower Bridge stood guard further downstream.

'Where do they live?' Pia asked. She'd been reluctant to check. It felt like stalking.

'Up in the sky.' Ed pointed across the bridge to the sparkling Shard that cut into the night sky. Pia gawped at the tallest building in London, which cast its shadow like a sun dial during the day and glinted as a steel blade in the twilight.

'You're kidding,' Pia said. 'Don't those apartments cost tens of millions of pounds?'

'I did say the fool had money to burn.'

Pia squeaked back in the Mini's leather seat, her mouth agog. The wealth of Cate's circle of friends and relatives was sobering, and she sat dumb for the rest of the drive.

The Shard's lift took a whole minute to reach the top floors. Rafe's flat occupied a corner of the building so that the floor to ceiling windows revealed the river and a domineering view over the city. The Gherkin and other landmarks were reduced to the scale of the ordinary below the wisps of eerie clouds that floated below Pia and Ed's feet.

Pia squashed her nose against the window. 'This is nuts.'

'Sleeping in the clouds is rather romantic though, don't you think,' Ed said with her lips pressed against the window.

Pia muttered her agreement. It was a child's dream to have a den like this. But its unattainable exclusivity made her nauseous. It wasn't out of jealousy or disapproval. Leagues scparated someone like Pia and Rafe, and it was an unscalable chasm that Pia would have to cross if she was ever to have a chance with Cate.

She twirled away from the window, with a numb white nose, and studied the luxury apartment. Furnishing was sparse and the room was dominated by its top-end light oak flooring. A group of anonymous low-level square sofas sat in the corner, and a glossy kitchen of black cabinets and large island was spread at the back. The rear wall had two pictures by Warhol—multiple Marilyns and bananas—and a nude woman made from ebony reclined by the sofas.

'It's not Cate though is it,' Pia muttered. She found it unfathomable that she lived in this characterless luxury box. Pia peeped towards a door that allowed a glimpse into a low-lit bedroom. The thought of what must happen in there made her feel ill and she tore away her gaze.

Ed cleared her throat. 'I'm sure she'll make an impression on it at some point, if she wants to.'

The apartment was beginning to fill with people that Pia recognised and their partners that she did not. Denise burst in grinning from ear to ear.

'I brought a karaoke box,' she squealed, holding a microphone in the air for anyone to see who doubted her.

'Lord save us,' Ed grumbled and Pia at least smiled at Denise's enthusiasm. They watched Rafe bound over and congratulate Denise on her fabulous idea and wrestle the karaoke machine to a prominent position by the windows for all of London to see.

'I suppose I'd better go and say hello to the silly tit,' Ed said, and she left Pia to swirl her glass of white wine alone.

The bedroom door caught Pia's attention as it opened wider. Cate stepped out, refined in a black dress, her hair tied up in a swirl to reveal her elegant neck. Her arms were bare and she looked like royalty as she reached out to greet a guest, her face a perfect picture of serenity and cordiality.

Pia glared down at her drink and swirled it round the glass, embarrassed to see her well-worn trainers ripple through the liquid. She was tempted to abandon her drink and leave, but when she glanced up Cate was staring at her. Cate waved and broke into a beaming grin. Her expression was full of relief and joy at the sight of Pia.

Pia's discomfort and self-consciousness of a moment ago evaporated and she found herself smiling without restraint and her cheeks glowing. Cate skipped towards her, almost breaking into a run, and Pia moved to greet her.

Cate stopped a foot away. Both of them leaned together, Cate seeming as eager as Pia to close even this small gap.

'Hi.' Cate gazed into her eyes. Her face was soft in the dim light, and Pia could feel her warmth against her cheek.

'Hi,' Pia whispered. She was transfixed by the look on Cate's face and her dark eyes.

'I didn't know if you'd come,' Cate breathed. 'I'm so glad you have.'

She slipped her fingers between Pia's, and Pia felt her insides thrill at the sensation of their touch. As their fingers entwined and palms moulded together, Pia's arm fluttered with delight.

'Let me get you some Champagne.' Cate's voice was hypnotic. 'I know it's the one luxury you have a weakness for. I bought some Billecart-Salmon for you.'

Pia followed, entranced and submissive to Cate's wishes. As Cate leaned down to the drinks cooler, Pia's eyes seduced her body. She stroked the curve of her back and hips. She admired the light downy hair on her neck as she poured the bubbling drink. The temptation to lean forward and caress her neck with butterfly kisses was overwhelming. Her whole body longed to touch her.

Cate turned and gave Pia a flute. It was cool and wet in her fingers with the mist of condensation. Their fingers touched, soft and blazing against the cold drink. Pia sipped at the Champagne, bubbles prickling her lips and the icy liquid chilling her chest. But her body recovered in an instant, burning again for Cate's touch.

'I have to be the polite hostess for a while,' Cate whispered. She reached out and rested her fingertips on Pia's arm with the lightest of touches. 'Please don't go while I'm away.'

Her eyes lingered on Pia's and her lips parted as if she were about to say more. Pia opened her mouth in expectation, but all she could think was 'kiss me'. Open those lips and kiss me. Run your tongue inside my mouth and slide your lips over mine. Tear off my shirt and tease my nipples between your fingers. Spread me naked over your luxurious kitchen island. Lick and devour me and don't stop until I scream.

Pia gulped and nodded, and Cate sauntered into the room. Her pupils were dark as she looked back over her shoulder. When the party consumed her, Pia breathed out.

'Oh God.'

18

Pia's arousal and emotional high ebbed as the rest of the room came into focus. Then it drained away completely when she noticed Ed analysing her over her spectacles.

She strolled up to Pia. 'So, are you having a good time shortarse?'

Pia mumbled something that wasn't coherent when it left her brain let alone after it had been mangled by her tongue. She took several generous sips of champagne in an attempt to cover up her unintelligibility. 'Think I need another drink.' She set her glass on a curving, modern-classic dining table and grabbed a bottle of Champagne.

Ed frowned and touched the tabletop, stroking along its glossy veneer. 'You know, I'd bet good money this is an original Isokon.'

Pia examined it more closely. Its modern design suggested a purchase for a few thousand from the King's Road, but the wood had a tinge of ochre and wear that implied greater age.

'They're expensive aren't they?' Pia assumed they were.

'Some are museum pieces.' Ed slipped a coaster under Pia's glass. 'Got to give him credit. He does have some good taste.' And she glanced towards Cate who was being the gracious hostess on the other side of the room.

Pia glugged her second glass and refilled it.

'Have you seen their wedding photos by the way?' Ed enquired.

Pia's heart sank. 'No. I haven't seen the wedding pictures.'

'There's a copy somewhere.' Ed squeezed through bodies to a plush sideboard. Pia expected her to return with a leather-bound album, but she thrust into her hand a magazine.

'They were in *Hello*?' Pia said, in disbelief. 'Of course they were in *Hello*.' She was all the more dejected and the magazine felt repellent in her hands.

'Aren't you going to look?' Ed nudged her. 'I thought you'd be interested in the photographs.'

With reluctance Pia flicked open the magazine that naturally fell to a double-page spread of Rafe and Cate. Their airbrushed images and alarming white teeth smiled out at her. Rafe beamed and was dashing in his morning suit. Cate was stunning. She had on a simple, elegant dress, and flowers in her hair was all that were needed to make it sublime. Pia stared into the image of Cate's eyes and didn't recognise her there. Perhaps the airbrushing had worn her away. Pia begrudged reading the caption and gave up when she understood they'd married at Kensington Palace.

'There's more. Flick over the page.'

What followed was even more nauseating: Cate and Rafe's honeymoon. The main photograph showed them gazing at a twilight ocean from their exclusive villa balcony on the island of Mustique. Cate wore a light dress and her face was turned away. Rafe stood behind her, commanding the picture, his shirt undone to the waist and his strong arms holding her like a vice. His masculinity and wealth dripped from the photo.

Pia handed back the magazine and refilled her glass once more. 'Very nice,' she mumbled.

Ed frowned at her the entire time that it took Pia to drain her glass. 'I didn't take you for a big drinker. How many glasses have you had?'

'M'not,' Pia noticed that her mouth felt rather numb and clumsy around the words.

'How many glasses shortarse?'

'Losssst count.' Pia stared at the one she held. ''scuse me. Think I need some air.'

She filled her glass and wandered aimlessly, and incompetently, across the room. The closest she could find to fresh air was the great window over London.

She leant her head against the glass. 'Well...' she sighed. 'Bugger.'

What was she doing here lusting after someone so beyond her? She lifted her glass to her lips and slurped without removing her head from the window. She was not feeling well, but more alcohol was irresistible at that moment.

'Can I have your attention everyone!' Rafe's voice boomed across the room and the chatter faded. Pia stumbled around and blinked to focus. Rafe leapt onto the precious dining table, his shoes clattering on the surface. His large, muscular presence seemed to fill the room.

'That's better,' he shouted. 'I can see everyone now. I wanted to thank you all for coming this evening. We have the editorial for the first edition bang on time, and all we're missing is a photograph of the team. So in a few minutes I've organised something a little bit special for the inside front cover of *Bennet* no. 1. Hold on to your hats.' He leapt off the table.

'Flash bastard,' Pia heard someone mutter nearby. She turned to see one of the young subeditors gossiping to another. 'Do you know he bought this place off plan? Didn't even bother with a viewing. He throws several million around as if he's buying groceries.'

Pia was beginning to feel sick of the sound of money, and no doubt a bit sick from the alcohol. She lurched around the room, asking for the loo, and at someone's direction stumbled into a short corridor behind the kitchen.

She pushed open the heavy bathroom door and leant back against it. It eased shut behind her and sealed out the noise of the party. She sighed, free from the constant reminder of riches.

'Oh that's better.' Her body relaxed. The stress and strain flowed down her limbs and dissipated, leaving her light and euphoric from the champagne. 'Much better.' She lifted her glass and enjoyed the cool sparkling liquid on her lips. But her head was spinning. Giddy, she opened her eyes, but then she became quite irate.

'Oh come on,' she said exasperated.

The room was white smoky marble from the floor to the ceiling. The bowl itself was unassuming white pottery and suspended from the wall. But to its side was another full-height window with London resplendent beneath it. Even the bog had a multi-million-pound view and was more prime real estate than any house Pia would ever own.

'This is taking the piss,' she slurred.

She guzzled the last of the Champagne and clinked the glass down on the marble. She stomped over to the window and glared down.

'Who the hell thinks London should see their arse on the loo?'

She surveyed the city below, its gleaming spires built from money made from money, and thought of all the financiers that spent the millions from millions on things as stupid as a loo with a view. She had an irresistible urge to shout at London. She wanted to raise two fingers to it and not at all in victory.

But instead, with her new habit, she twirled round, pulled down her trousers and bared her best asset. And if she could have peed down a drain pipe of the Shard she would have done.

For a drunken moment it was satisfying. She showed London exactly what she thought of its exclusive city. But a strange and loud sound pulsed outside the window. It was like something powerful chopping into the air at high speed. She could feel it throbbing through her whole body. She peeped over her shoulder.

There was a helicopter hovering outside. It was a little distance from the building, but the pilot was quite clear. There was also an additional person with what appeared to be a camera.

Above the chopper noise she heard a cheer from the main room.

'What the…?

She struggled with her trousers. With no small amount of panic she tripped and shuffled away from the window. She wrestled with her zip to more cheering from inside the apartment. When she opened the door, the entire team was standing by the window with glasses raised for a group photo.

Rafe spotted her exit from the toilet. 'Pia! Come on. You're missing the team photo.'

'Oh no.' She bowed her head and her shoulders slumped. She sloped towards the happy group, hoping that indeed she had missed the photo.

—

Pia sat in the corner, inconsolable, incomprehensible and dribbling a small amount of wine down her chin. She'd have to wait until morning to see if the photographer had caught her best cheek. She gawped at the reclining nude beside the sofa, tempted to prostrate herself across it, just to end the night with a little more humiliation.

'Pia?' A gentle voice called her.

She lifted her head to see Cate's concerned face. Cate sat beside her and held her arm. Her thighs squeezed unbearably soft and warm into Pia's.

'Are you OK?' Cate whispered.

'Fine. Jusssst fine.' Although inebriated, Pia must have communicated her desolation through some subtle use of slurring.

'Please tell me what's wrong.'

Pia breathed in, thought very carefully about what she wanted to say, and then said, 'Ufff.'

Cate slipped her fingers through Pia's and squeezed. 'Please tell me. You look so unhappy.'

Pia inhaled once more. 'It's jussst. I know that I said I could understand you a bit now.' She blinked, slow and heavy, trying on focus on Cate. 'And why you wanted money. But now, I can see just how far off I was. Now I really know why you didn't choose me. Thasss all.'

Cate's fingers twitched.

'I can see just how sssstupid I was to fall for you. And it makes me feel a bit little, and a bit crap.'

'Pia, it wasn't like that.' She reached round to hold Pia's arms and forced her to look straight into her eyes. 'Yes, I won't deny that financial security was attractive for me. But I'd made enormous commitments. There were so many people depending on me.'

Pia gulped and turned away. She was unwilling and unable to say anything.

'You mustn't be like this,' Cate implored. 'I hate that I've made you feel inadequate, because it's so unjustified.'

Cate dropped to her knees and grabbed Pia's hands. 'You are the most incredible person I've ever met Pia. You're beautiful, intelligent, talented, and the way you see the world has been so revealing for me. The way you discern the worth in things, and people, is so special. Your respect for them is humbling. Please don't be wrong about yourself. Don't under-estimate how wonderful you are.'

Pia stared at her, uncomprehending.

'You see the nugget of gold in everyday things that others pass without a second thought. If there was a tramp lying on the street, stinking to high heaven, you'd be the one who noticed him hugging his dog to keep it warm.'

Cate glanced down for a moment.

'I hadn't been feeling good about myself for a long time. I didn't realise, but I'd made some poor choices and misjudged what was important to me. I didn't like the person I was becoming. And that night, that perfect night, when I asked you to describe what you saw in front of you. When you said I was beautiful and kind it almost broke my heart. I was so moved that that's how you saw me and I wanted to be that person.'

She gazed at Pia, tears glistening in her eyes.

'I've made some terrible choices. But you cherish the things that make life worth living and I love you for it.'

For a moment, Pia heard nothing but Cate's voice, those melodious tones that had charmed her from the start. Her last sentence echoed in her consciousness and tugged at her heart. She focused on the deep pools of Cate's eyes, seeing the true woman again.

It was a pity the moment was shattered by a loud screech of feedback on the karaoke speaker. Rafe's voice boomed on the microphone. 'Wham!'

It would have puzzled Pia at the best of times. A second later, everyone else nodded in understanding when the drums and bass guitar to *I'm Your Man* pounded the room.

Cate stood up looking horrified as Rafe launched into an unbridled version of the song. He sought her in the crowd as he sang. He found her in time for the chorus, when he pointed his finger at her and screamed out the title words.

Cate went pale and, without a word, left the room. All eyes followed her except those of Rafe. He glanced at the lyrics and before he could look up again his vanity was saved by an enthusiastic Denise. She leapt up to grab another microphone and joined in with gusto.

And although the entire evening was hazy at best, that was definitely the last Pia remembered of it.

19

It was possible that Pia woke herself up with her own snore. But it was also possible that it might have been someone else's. She opened her heavy eyelids and found that, as she suspected, she was face down in a pillow, her cheek and nose mashed into the fabric. She squashed her cheek to the side and squinted in the bright light, which in turn made her wince with the pain of an evil headache.

'Ugh,' she murmured. Even that slight movement made her nauseous. She gnashed her mouth open and shut and tried to revive her dry and shrivelled tongue. She had a feeling she might have been sick, but she wasn't sure where. At least it wasn't in the rich white cotton sheets that she lay in, wherever they were.

She heard the flick of a newspaper beside her and with a heavy sense of dread, and a well-founded fear of vomiting, she twisted round her head.

'Hello darling,' Ed said, all lightness and cheer. She was sat up in bed with a broadsheet. She regarded Pia over her glasses with a wry smile. Pia's eyes wandered lower and she noticed that, underneath the fold of the silk dressing gown, Ed was quite naked. The side of a freckled breast lay exposed.

With a rising sense of panic Pia delved beneath the sheets. There, she found her own naked breasts, tummy and smooth behind. When Ed raised her eyebrows, Pia realised she was staring in horror.

'We didn't…?'

'Well we tried, but I'm afraid you weren't up to much,' Ed replied with a nonchalant flick of a page.

Despite her thunderous hangover, Pia still managed to be piqued by the dismissal.

'And we need to go shopping.' Ed looked stern. 'You seriously need a map to the G spot.'

Pia blushed and found herself absent-mindedly testing the tackiness of her fingers. 'But, but, not everybody is that fond of being touched, there.'

Ed shrugged.

'And I might not have wanted to have gone…' Pia felt uneasy and queasy, '…delving, if you didn't seem keen?'

'Oh I agree darling. Everyone has different tastes and fetishes for every area. Dip your finger in some lube and then between one person's buttocks and they're in heaven. Another, hell. Some just like a bit of warning.'

Pia's chin dropped and she involuntarily clenched her bottom.

Ed reached out and held her hand. 'Darling?'

'Yes?'

'You must learn when I'm pulling your leg.' Ed laughed. 'Although I'd rather you didn't because this is far too much fun. You fell asleep and were as useless as a dildo made of jelly.'

Pia let her face fall back into the pillow with relief.

'And as if I'd want to sleep with your skinny derrière,' Ed added.

Pia lifted up her head. 'Why am I naked then?'

'You insisted and I wasn't going to object.' Ed returned to her paper. 'Nice cheeks by the way.'

If Pia could have thrown the pillow at her without simultaneously vomiting she would have done.

Ed laughed. 'I'd recognise that bottom anywhere now. Including the company photograph.'

'Oh no.'

Ed raised her eyebrows and nodded. When Pia only stared at her with alarm, Ed thumbed over her phone and threw it on the mattress.

Pia stared at the glowing image: a group of small happy shining faces cheering in one window of the Shard, and a shining white arse in the next.

Pia fell into the pillow and moaned, 'I want to die.'

—

Pia sat up in bed and managed to clothe herself in knickers and T-shirt by the time Ed returned with a steaming cup of fresh ground coffee.

'Thank you.' Pia inhaled the restorative aroma. She took tiny sips, nothing too taxing for her fractious digestive system.

Ed swung her legs on to the bed and turned to Pia. 'So. Do you want to talk about it?'

'About what?' Pia said through a sip.

'Being in love with Cate.'

'Oh.' The cool dread of being found out flooded Pia's insides. 'How did you know?'

'Honestly.' Ed rolled her eyes. 'Who could miss those yearning puppy dog eyes when she comes in the room? Although, so far, it does seem to have evaded Rafe, luckily for you. What's going on?'

'Nothing,' Pia said dejected. But she had the nagging feeling of missing something important. She remembered Cate, holding her arms, imploring her. She had the sensation of being lifted by sweet poignant words, being cherished by someone grabbing her by the heart and talking directly to her soul. But she was buggered if she could remember what she'd said.

'It's not one-sided is it?' Ed asked.

'There's nothing going on now.'

'What happened?'

Pia breathed out defeated. 'We met the night before her wedding. We spent hours together. Precious hours. And then...'

'Had sex.'

Pia nodded. 'Wonderful, lovely sex.'

'Oh Pia.' Ed looked pained and sympathetic. 'I must admit I'm surprised. I didn't think Cate was the last fling sort.'

'It wasn't like that.' Pia snapped. 'It wasn't like a one-night stand.' She frowned trying to communicate the easy rapport, the excitement of the night, the fluidity in which they came together. 'It was like spending weeks with anyone else. It was magic. Perfect.'

Ed pursed her lips in pained disbelief. 'And you expected her to give up everything after one night?'

Pia gulped. She felt stupid and emotional.

Ed reached out and held her hand. 'You can't expect someone who's about to get married, with relatives, friends, the groom all waiting at the church, to walk away. Coupled with starting a new business together, Cate had far too much invested. You can't expect someone like that to drop everything and believe in love at first sight.'

'But I do. Because that's what happened to me.' A single hot tear streamed down Pia's cheek. 'I was hooked from the first time I saw her, and everything that happened afterwards made me love her more. I would have done anything for her.'

'Oh shortarse.' Ed buried a sniffling Pia into her bosom to console her. 'I know. I believe you. I've seen the way you look at her and quite frankly the way she looks at you. And I'd walk over hot coals for a love like that.'

20

The week after passed in a whirlwind of ferocious activity as the magazine prepared to go to press. Ed sent Pia criss-crossing over London to snap last-minute photos and Rafe and Cate were rarely in the office, and never together.

Late one evening in the *Bennet* building, after an opening night outside the Theatre Royal, Pia spotted Cate staring out of the window in a small side office. She could see her in the black glass, her face reflected against the sparkling lights of the city. She seemed tired and drawn. When Pia caught her gaze she turned around and her face lifted.

'Hey.' Cate's was quiet. 'You're a sight for sore eyes.'

Pia beamed at her words and skipped into the office to stand beside her. 'Hi.' She drew up close.

'What have you been up to Pia Benitez-Smith? I bet you have some escapade to cheer me up.'

Pia considered for a moment. 'Today, Ed sent me to photograph the men's changing rooms in Selfridges, where it is alleged that a certain MP changed more than clothes with a young assistant.'

'And how did that go?'

'Well. I didn't realise there was anyone in the changing rooms. I managed to capture the rapper Davey Silver Rock down to his boxers.'

'Oh dear.' Cate's lips twitched in the corners.

'I had no idea who he was.' Pia shrugged. 'But his bodyguards were quite insistent about seeing me to the door. Very nice men. Carried me all the way.'

Cate laughed. 'Only you Benitez-Smith.' She smiled at her, not letting go of her eyes. 'I've missed you.'

They stood a few inches apart, close enough to feel each other's presence.

Cate broke into a grin. 'At least I now have a photo of you to keep me company.'

Pia slapped her hands to her face and emitted a muffled groan from behind her fingers. 'That bloody photo.'

Cate's delivery was deadpan. 'It shows a side of you most people don't see.'

'Oh, don't.' Pia cringed at the memory of seeing a poster-size print of the team photo on Ed's wall, complete with Pia's contribution from the bathroom window.

Cate's soft fingers slipped between Pia's face and hand, and enticed her arm down to her side.

'Sorry. I couldn't resist.' Cate's face was full of amusement and sparkle. 'Made my day on a very gloomy one.'

Pia could feel Cate's warmth through her dress as she held her hand to her thigh. Pia's chest filled with longing. She gazed into Cate's eyes and saw tenderness and admiration there. She was lost trying to fathom Cate's thoughts and didn't realise that she drew closer still.

Cate blinked and looked down. 'I'm trying to sort things out,' she whispered. 'I need a little time. It hasn't been going very well, as you might imagine.' She drew Pia's hand to her chest. 'Please give me a chance.'

Pia's response was stifled by a loud cough from the doorway.

'Pia.' Ed peeped around the door. 'I'm afraid I need to send you on another errand.'

Cate let her hand slip. 'I need to go home anyway.' Her vitality drained away as she said the words. 'Good night both.' And without glancing at either, she left the room.

Pia's mouth must have made a perfect 'o' shape as she gawped at the door.

Ed pursed her lips together and drummed her fingers on the doorframe. 'What was that about shortarse?'

Pia shook her head, in an attempt to inspire her brain, but it didn't work. Her heart beat so hard that it deafened her ears and distracted from any coherent thought. 'I don't know.'

Ed glared at her. 'You could have at least given me an honest lie and said it was about her birthday party.'

Pia stared at Ed with eyes as round as her mouth. 'Seriously, I don't know.'

'Hmmm.' Ed turned to leave. 'By the way, are you ready with a posh frock for tomorrow evening?'

'Huh?' said Pia, her brain still less than fully functional.

Ed peered over her glasses, 'For Cate's birthday bash dear?'

'Oh, is there a dress code?'

'It's black tie darling.'

'It's black tie?' Pia's shoulders slumped and every last bit of breath escaped her in a sigh. 'Of course it's black tie.'

—

Her mother's bottom was all that was visible, poking out of the bedroom wardrobe. Hangers rattled from within as clothes were thrust from side to side with determination.

'You try this one.' A black garment flew through the air to Pia who stood self-conscious in her bra and briefs.

'What is it?' Pia stretched the fabric with her fingertips as if it was something unpleasant.

Her mother's red face swept up from the cupboard.

177

'It's a dress mija. Remember? You wore one when you were three, and it made you cry.'

'I mean, how on earth do I put it on?' Pia said, unable to fathom the entrance to the item.

'Give it here.' Her mother shook the material out and lovingly smoothed the little black dress down her own body. 'Oh, I was so slim and beautiful back then.' She looked mournful. 'You try it.' And she held it up against Pia.

'OK.' Pia sulked.

She pulled the stretchy material over her head, hunched her shoulders and pouted. She squinted in the mirror and was even less impressed than she anticipated.

'I look like I'm in drag.'

'Don't be stupid. You're like a teenager who's been asked to do the dishes. Now stand up straight.' She squeezed Pia's arms. 'God gave you beautiful breasts. Stand up and be proud of them, instead of walking around like they're cow's udders.'

'Mama. It's just this dress.'

'Come on. Titties out.' Her mother pushed her shoulders back. 'There.' She puffed her own chest out with pride. 'There's my beautiful girl.'

Pia scowled into the mirror. She looked passable, if not at all happy.

'It's nice mama, and I know you were gorgeous in it. But it's not me and I really need to look the part for this thing.'

Her mother regarded her from beneath her eyebrows and put her arms around the back of Pia's neck.

'What you doing with this married lady, Pia? Why you trying to dress to impress? Heh?'

'It's not like that. I just don't want to be an embarrassment.'

Her mother's expression wasn't at all convinced.

Pia was downcast. 'Nothing's going to happen. She's married. She's working for his magazine.'

Her mother breathed out. 'So why do you go to this party then?'

Pia swallowed and peeped up. The words were difficult because they were the truth. 'Because I love her and I can't do anything else.'

'Oh mija.' Her mother drew her under her arm and rocked her from side to side. Pia closed her eyes and was smothered and warmed by the embrace.

'Let's hope nothing does happen, heh?' her mother said. 'Imagine the mess you'd be in then.'

'Nothing will.'

Her mother stroked her hair. 'If you say.'

And Pia did her best to smile.

'Now.' Her mother released Pia and clapped her hands together. 'We have one more thing to try.'

She knelt by the bed and eased out a dust cover from beneath the mattress. 'This', she said, zipping around the edge, 'was your father's.' She magicked out a dinner jacket with slim trousers and held them up to Pia. 'It may work with a nip and a tuck.'

Pia's breasts filled the shirt where a man's broad chest had been, and her mother pinned back the folds of spare material to mould the shirt around her tummy. The trousers were a surprisingly good fit and, with some more judicious pinning, her mother tailored the jacket into a more feminine line. As an afterthought, her mother slicked back Pia's hair with water and drew her towards the mirror.

Pia stared at her svelte image in the reflection. Her wet hair, tight around her head, enhanced her slim features. Pia's eyes appeared more beautiful and defined. Her mother had tucked and curved the suit around her so that there was no doubt about the gender of the person inside.

Her mother drew her fingers to her mouth in prayer. 'Oh mija.'

Pia blushed when she saw her mother's tearful admiration. 'Will it do mama?'

Her mother pulled her close and kissed her on the cheek. 'I've never seen a more beautiful woman.'

21

'Ed?'

Pia had been following a tall, elegant lady across the gravel to the entrance of Sir Charles' house. The woman had swept-back grey hair and was dressed in a long flowing cloak: a striking appearance. When the woman twirled round, a version of Ed with contact lenses and a flourish of makeup stared at her.

'Ed. You're stunning.' Pia beamed.

'Well look at you shortarse,' Ed replied. She gestured for Pia to twirl. 'It's not as if you're ever hard on the eye, but you scrub up deliciously.' She swirled Pia round and looked her up and down with more than a little admiration. 'You know, if I were twenty years younger…' She considered for a moment. 'That's bollocks, I would have you now if you weren't so in love with that Cate woman.'

Pia laughed and offered an arm to the sophisticated lady who towered above her. 'Shall we?'

'We shall.' Ed grinned.

The entrance hall sparkled with chandelier lights and chatter filled the air. People crossed to and fro with a ripple of a gown or cloak. The full, resonant sound of a live jazz band playing *The Very Thought of You* echoed through from the ballroom and Pia felt like she'd entered a different world. Someone squeezed their fingers around Pia's arm and she spun round to see Lady Wynne.

'Pia, you look dashing this evening.' Lady Wynne smiled.

Whether it was because of the whiff of Champagne in the air or the feeling of confidence that her suit imbued, Pia kissed Lady Wynne on both cheeks.

'Thank you for inviting me.'

'It's a pleasure. Cate has such a high regard for you and Ed. I'm overjoyed to see you both.'

'Well I'm glad to hear it,' Ed said with customary confidence and a wry smile.

'Oh yes. She's very fond of you and respects you too. Which is more than I can say for some of the numpties here. Some of the ones she knows through Rafe, I don't know.' She rolled her eyes.

Lady Wynne took Pia by one arm and Ed by the other. 'Let me welcome you properly. Let's get you a drink.'

They were met in the ballroom by waiters with Champagne. Lady Wynne handed them bubbling glasses and ushered them through to a quieter spot at the back of the ballroom. Pia glanced over the crowd, congregating in polite circles and sporadically breaking into loud guffaws.

Wynne placed her hand on Pia's arm. 'Cate will be down in a few moments. She's just getting dressed. It's been a stressful day for her, so I'm sure she'll be eager to relax with you two.'

'Wynne!' The irate and deep voice of Sir Charles couldn't avoid being heard. 'Where's Lady Wynne?'

'Here dear.' Wynne waved in the air with an irritated flourish.

Sir Charles' large frame and ruddy face burst through the mass. 'Ah Wynne. Where the hell is Cate? Intolerable to be late to your own party.'

'Rubbish. She needn't turn up at all. That's her prerogative.'

Sir Charles made a noise not unlike a horse snorting. 'Well. I'm not at all impressed with her today.'

'Later my dear. Let's all just try to behave with some decorum for the duration of the party.'

Sir Charles ruffled his shoulders and cleared his throat before Pia caught his attention. 'Ah, Peter. Well, good to see you here at least.'

'Peter?' Ed said. 'Who the hell's Peter?' Further inquiry was stifled by a gentle but firm elbow to Ed's ribs from Lady Wynne.

'Has Wynne got you drinking Champagne?' Sir Charles looked appalled. 'Let's get you a real drink. You there,' he bellowed towards a waiter. 'Get a large Talisker for this man. Or are you more of a Speyside kind of chap?'

'Talisker's fine,' Pia replied in her deepest voice.

Ed had crossed her arms and was querying her with an eyebrow. The whisky was prompt and Pia began to glug it out of terror.

'I'm trying to find Cate's friend Toby,' Sir Charles continued. 'Do you know the fellow?'

'Me?' Pia said a couple of octaves too high. She dropped her chin onto her chest and growled. 'No. Sorry. I don't.'

'Oh.' Sir Charles peered around. 'Stupid fellow has just bought a two-hundred acre estate and he hasn't got the first idea about countryside management. I promised to show him his way round a shotgun. The sissy's never fired one in his life.'

'Perhaps another time might be more appropriate.' Lady Wynne held his arm. 'This is Cate's party. I much prefer to spend birthdays without the sound of accidental gunshot.'

'Well. If the girl ever shows up…' Sir Charles turned back and for the first time he seemed to notice all three of them. 'Well, Peter, are you going to introduce me to your lady friend?'

It took a moment or two for Pia to register who he meant. She spluttered her apology and gestured towards her companion.

'Sir Charles, this is my boss, Ed.'

'Ed?' Sir Charles snapped. 'What the hell kind of name is that for a woman?'

'A better one than Peter,' Ed replied, and she matched Sir Charles' firm handshake.

Pia stared at Ed with alarm and tilted her whisky glass to her lips with a nervous twitch.

'That's the spirit my boy.' Sir Charles slapped her between the shoulder blades so that the air spat out of her lungs. 'Let's get you another.' And he swung round to find a waiter.

'Thanks,' Pia wheezed.

'Take it easy shortarse,' Ed said behind her hand. 'I've seen you on half a bottle of pop and it wasn't pretty.'

Sir Charles turned back, disgust wrinkling his features. 'Being bossed around by a woman, Peter? Good god man. Show her what you're made of.'

Ed smiled. 'I've seen what Peter's made of, and it's not quite what you think.'

Between the downed whisky and Ed's remark, Pia's heart went into palpitations. 'Another drink would be good,' she said, her deep voice breaking a little.

'Good. Good.' Sir Charles passed her the glass that had been delivered in haste by a nervous waiter. 'Drink up. You don't want to be a pussy.'

'No,' Ed said. 'I wouldn't want you to be a pussy. Just a part of you.'

'Jesus Ed,' Pia whispered.

Lady Wynne coughed and took Sir Charles' arm. 'Come on dear. Let's allow these two to enjoy the party. I'm sure Peter is man enough to find drinks on his own.'

'What?' Sir Charles barked. 'Yes of course, of course.' They faced the crowd into which Sir Charles bellowed, 'Ah, Toby! There you are. I must take you to the gun room.' And they disappeared into the throng.

Pia gasped out and almost flopped to the floor with the release of tension.

'Now shortarse.' Ed held her hands on her hips. 'How the bloody hell did you get into that mess?'

'It's a long story.' Pia wiped her brow. 'But please play along. He's a terrible bigot and I'd rather he thought I was a bloke than a lesbian.'

'Oh man up, Peter.' Ed snorted. 'He can't be that bad. You need to grow a pair sometimes. Quite literally if you're going to pull that off.'

Pia implored her. 'He's a very unpleasant man, and one that owns a bloody shotgun. In fact several by the sound of it.'

Ed laughed and patted her arm. 'Keep your boxers on shortarse.' And Ed took a swig of her Champagne. When the glass reached full tilt she stopped as if she'd spotted something startling. She lowered it slowly as her mouth dropped in unison.

'What?' Pia asked. She stretched up on tip-toes to see what had caught Ed's eye.

'Oh dear,' Ed whispered.

'What?'

Ed gulped and turned to look at Pia, a serious expression on her face. 'If I were you, I would avoid Cate this evening.'

'Why? What's happened?'

Ed didn't have a chance to reply. Pia followed the line of Ed's gaze, trying to peer over the heads of the crowd. And then the bodies parted and Pia had clear sight of Cate gliding towards them.

She wore a dress that covered enough for modesty but teased at Pia's imagination relentlessly. With every step, the diaphanous fabric of her silver dress flowed around her legs. A slit revealed naked skin almost to her hip. It winked for a moment before the glimpse was cruelly taken away. The neckline plunged to her waist, the beginning of the tantalising curve of her breasts visible. With Pia's fervent imagination, she may as well have been naked.

Cate smiled as she waved to a group of people. She mouthed an excuse to another. Then her eyes met Pia's.

She stopped in the middle of the room. The light in her eyes, a vestige from her polite smiles for her guests, turned dark. Pia had never witnessed such an intense look of longing as she saw in Cate. She couldn't move.

Cate approached, never removing her gaze from Pia. They drew together irresistibly and stood close, not uttering a word. Pia glowed with desire. She could feel her skin respond with arousal and craving. Her heart beat slow and strong and her chest rose with deep hot breaths. She could see Cate's breasts rise and fall with the same passionate force.

Pia's mouth fell open. Her fingers released her glass without thought, and it fell into the hands of Ed who slipped away from the entranced pair.

The lights were dimmed and the room filled with more bodies. The gentle sway of the slow jazz mesmerised and sedated the crowd. People flowed around them and still Pia could not take her eyes from Cate. As people streamed around the room, those who wanted to dance, those who wanted to watch and those who wanted to drink, Cate and Pia remained unmoved in the middle of the eddies of dancing couples.

Cate raised her hand and, no longer aware of their surroundings, Pia gently met it with her yearning fingers. The touch was thrilling. Pins and needles of pleasure danced through her arm and filled her body with arousal. She slipped her hand around Cate's back and the sensation of bare soft skin made her gasp.

'I can't.' Pia's voice was strangled. She pulled away, but Cate held her firm. 'I can't trust myself,' Pia said in desperation.

'You don't need to.' Cate's words were as good as a gentle caress down Pia's breasts and between her legs.

Pia quivered with both arousal and distress. 'Where's Rafe?'

'He's not coming.' Cate's eyes didn't waver for a second.

She rested her hand on Pia's shoulder and slowly swayed her hips to the music. Pia could feel her body undulate beneath her hand. Slow and seductive, Cate closed the gap. The lightest touch between them made Pia tremble with shocks of excitement. Breasts against breasts, nipples teasing nipples, legs sliding between legs.

Pia's breath was short, just an inch away from Cate's ear. 'You can't do this to me.'

Cate's lips stroked her cheek and she whispered, 'I've been wanting nothing else.'

Her breasts rose and fell, passionately caressing Pia's with every deep inhalation so that waves of tingling pleasure pulsed through Pia's body.

'Please,' Pia begged. 'You've no idea what you're doing to me.'

Cate didn't breathe a word. She reached behind her back and slipped Pia's hand over her hips.

Pia's fingers inflamed as they stroked over Cate's curves. The silky material slid over Cate's body with no resistance and Pia realised that Cate was completely naked beneath her dress. The thought of being able to slip her finger around the slit of the dress, around her thigh and into her warm hair made her groan.

'Seriously.' Pia gulped. 'If you kissed me….'

Cate stopped, her eyes wide and intense. Her hand slid from Pia's shoulder and she turned away. For a moment Pia thought she might be abandoning her, and then she felt Cate's urgent fingers pull her through the crowd.

22

'No-one will find us here,' Cate said.

She pulled Pia into the half-light of the mediaeval bedroom. The door slammed and fans of swords rattled on the wooden panelling. They stood for a moment, dark eyes staring, expectant lips parted, chests heaving with passion.

Cate swept forward. Her lips were hot and keen over Pia's mouth. Cate's hands were eager, seeking Pia's breasts as she swept her backwards, crashing into the wall. Cate devoured her. She kissed across Pia's lips, cheeks, down her neck, all the time squeezing her breasts in rhythm.

'Harder,' Pia breathed.

Cate stroked her breasts into her palms and, with a knowing deftness, her fingers and thumbs pinched her nipples. Thrilling spasms of excitement charged through Pia's breasts again and again as Cate pinched and teased her. Pia stared at her, overwhelmed by a piquant mix of fear and arousal as Cate pinched her harder than she ever dared desire.

When Pia groaned with exquisite gratification, Cate's pupils flooded her eyes. The look on her face was predacious. She tugged at Pia's jacket and tore at her shirt. When Cate's fingers stroked inside the waistband of Pia's trousers, excitement sparked between her legs and she tensed and pulsed inside.

Pia floundered, left incapable from arousal. Cate pulled her around and walked her back towards the four-poster bed, all the while thrusting and rubbing between her legs.

Pia panted enraptured. Her trousers and boxers relented to Cate's insistent tearing and her abundant warm moisture slipped over her legs as Cate stripped them down.

Clumsy and disoriented from pure burning lust, Pia stumbled back. She reached out and her fingers found the thick woven curtains that hung round the bed. Cate savaged her with kisses. She nibbled and licked her neck, devoured her chest. She took Pia's nipple between her teeth and tongue and sucked her hard so that Pia almost blacked out from the arousal that pulsed deep inside every single part of her body.

She writhed in ecstasy, pulling at the curtains, which snapped one ring at a time with every convulsion of pleasure. Cate pushed her onto the bed and gorged herself on Pia's naked body, kissing her as she slipped down to her knees. As Pia relinquished any vestige of control, she felt Cate's soft fingers stroke either side of her clitoris. They slipped in her moisture and parted her short hair in readiness.

Cate's tantalising tongue lapped at the bottom of her lips. She dipped deep inside and Pia groaned. Her tongue ran agonisingly slowly around the top of her lips, and then Pia, insensible with anticipation, felt her clitoris being sucked between Cate's lips.

'Oh fuck,' Pia cried. She thrust herself into Cate's mouth. 'Fuck.'

Cate buried her face into her and Pia grasped her hair.

'Fuck!' Pia screamed.

She pulled Cate's head harder between her legs. Her body curled taut in ecstasy and she groaned a single loud note of insane pleasure.

'Oh my fucking god,' Pia gasped.

She fell back onto the bed exhausted. Her body hummed with satisfied delight from her core all the way to the tips of her fingers. Cate kissed her with the gentlest strokes of her lips, easing her down.

The door crashed open. The weapons on the panelling reverberated around the room and Pia's eyes shot open.

'What the blazes is going on in here?' shouted the unmistakeable voice of Sir Charles.

Pia's belly froze and panic constricted her heart. She couldn't see Sir Charles, but his shadow was cast by the corridor light onto the curtains at the end of the bed. His intimidating frame loomed large with a long erection. Pia recognised that long thin shape. It was Sir Charles' shotgun and he wouldn't be pleased to see her.

'Sir Charles!' Cate jumped to her feet and smoothed down her dress.

'Who devil's in there with you?' Sir Charles shouted. 'It better be Rafe.'

Pia's heart cantered in her chest and threatened to burst out of her ribs. Her skin burned with embarrassment and terror and she crouched on the bed ready to flee. If she'd been calm and collected she would have jumped off the bed with precision and sprinted for the door. But this was as far removed from collected as Pia had been in her life.

Like a terrified animal she leapt through the curtain. Her frantic form shrouded in the curtain flew through the air into the bulk of Sir Charles. Though slight in comparison, Pia's small body sprang with such velocity that the old knight was sent sprawling to the floor. As Pia landed on the irate gentlemen a deafening shot exploded over her head.

She heard Cate shout. 'Jesus Christ, that thing's loaded.'

Pia leapt to her feet and ran for the door. She sped down the corridor where she knew there were no loos and leapt onto the attic staircase. She spun, wide-eyed with panic, and watched the corridor. No-one yet followed and she crouched in the dark stairwell, her chest heaving.

'What the hell is going on?' Lady Wynne appeared at the top of the main stairs, her face red with indignation.

Sir Charles strode into view and bellowed 'There's a naked man loose in the house. A naked man with enormous breasts.'

Before a stunned Wynne could intervene, Sir Charles pounded down the corridor towards Pia, the shotgun still grasped in his hand.

'The coward ran this way,' he roared.

Pia's breath screamed through her teeth as she stared at the approaching knight.

'Charles. Charles!' Wynne shouted. 'For god's sake put that down. You could kill someone.'

But the tall man marched along the corridor, kicking open doors as he passed. Cate stumbled into the corridor and shrieked after her grandfather.

Pia whispered to herself. 'Fuck, fuck, fuck!' Her white fingers pinched the bannister. The gun-wielding avenger loomed and she had neither the presence of mind nor physical ability to speak out loud. Her legs sprang to life and she thumped up the wooden stairs to the attic.

'There's the bastard!' he shouted.

She glanced back to see Sir Charles' irate face glaring up at her. He pointed at her with the hand that still held the gun and to Pia's horror his fingers were still wrapped carelessly around the trigger.

With a last rush of adrenaline Pia thrust up the stairs as the boom of gunfire erupted beneath her. The air against her cheeks was hot with splinters and dust. Chippings needled her naked chest. She ducked as a great block of plaster hurtled down the stairwell to hit the floor behind her and shatter around Sir Charles.

In more or less one piece she landed with a barefooted thud on the attic floorboards. She pounded across the room. But that was all she could hear.

She slackened her pace. Her footsteps slowed but no sound rose above them. There were no shouts. There was no gunshot. No sound of any pursuit. Only shocking silence and the rhythm of her own rasping breath. She turned and faced the emptiness behind her.

The eerie stillness was broken by frantic steps and shuffling at the bottom of the stairs. Agitated voices spoke in short bursts of orders and concern. She could hear Lady Wynne's voice strident above them all.

Another fear took hold in her belly and a chill numbed her insides as she crept back through the darkness. She heard strained voices talking over one another and she forced herself to peer over the edge.

Sir Charles lay at the bottom of the staircase. White dust and chunks of plaster coated his chest and face, broken by a flow of vivid red blood across his forehead. His body lay unmoving beneath the flailing limbs of others.

'Call 999!'

'I think there's a pulse.'

'Is there a doctor?'

—

Pia sat hunched on the attic floor for what could have been minutes or hours. She focussed on the parallel floorboards that ran into the distance, her thoughts a mass of conflict.

'Pia?' She half-registered Cate's whisper. Her silhouette edged towards her. 'Pia?' Cate crouched down, and it was only when she held her hand that Pia surfaced.

'Is he dead?' Pia was almost sick with the words.

'No, no.' Cate half-laughed out of stress. 'He has a very nasty bump on his head, and he's confused. It is worrying, but he's not dead.'

Pia covered her mouth, her heavy breaths rasping between her fingers. 'What a mess.'

'He'll be fine. He's talking. It's going to be all right.' Cate squeezed her arms in reassurance.

'Such a mess.'

'I know.' Cate frowned. 'Why the hell didn't he put the gun down?'

Pia shivered.

'I brought your clothes.' Cate swept the jacket around Pia's shoulders and hugged her tight. Tears brimmed from Pia's eyes. She would have loved to have stayed warm and safe inside Cate's arms, but she had to push her away.

'I mean it's all such a mess,' Pia said.

Cate leant back and stared at her.

'What about Rafe?' Pia's voice was breaking.

'I'm leaving Rafe. I know I should have sorted everything first. I'm sorry. But I couldn't resist you tonight.' Cate implored her with her eyes. She reached out to touch Pia's cheek. 'Have you any idea how many times I've relived that night? I think of you every day. I imagine what it's like to hold you at night. When I saw you this evening, more beautiful than ever, I couldn't stay away.'

'But now what?' Pia looked up at her helpless.

She could see Cate's face in the dim light break into a loving smile. 'Whatever you want. We can do whatever you want.'

Pia tried to swallow away her emotion but her throat had clenched shut with despair. Every time she imagined life with Cate the image of her with Rafe on their honeymoon flashed in Pia's head. The image from the magazine of Rafe's toned body naked to the waist enveloping Cate was burned on her brain. She couldn't touch Cate without thinking how Rafe's hands had been there too. How easily she'd hopped from Rafe to Pia and back again.

'How would I ever trust you?'

'What?' Pia could hear dread in Cate's faint whisper.

'How could I ever trust you after all that's happened?'

Cate glanced down. 'I'm sorry, I couldn't walk away from the wedding, Rafe's family and friends and the job. It was too much all at once.' She peeped up at Pia. 'In retrospect, it would have been the right thing to do.'

Pia shook her head. 'But you were unfaithful to Rafe too. What's to stop that happening again?'

'Oh Pia.' Cate grabbed her hands. 'It wouldn't be like that. I would never be unfaithful to you. You must believe me.' Cate's distress was clear in her voice. 'I've never felt this way about Rafe. I've never had this passion and adoration, or respect for him. We were always more friends.'

Cate took a moment, as if to gather her thoughts. 'I have loved you since you fell out of that tree.' She breathed out in a laugh. 'I will always remember holding your face and gazing into your eyes. I was trying to check that you were well. But you peered back straight inside me. It was as if you knew everything about me in that second. It thrilled and scared me, but looking back, that was the moment.'

Pia couldn't speak. Tears rolled down her cheeks.

Cate beamed at her, love evident across every feature. 'That night was magical. I tried to persuade myself that it was only special because it was transient. But everything you've done since, everything I've seen of you, has made me love you more. I adore you Pia Benitez-Smith. I've loved you since you fell out of that tree and I will love you for the rest of my life.'

The words sank into Pia with such a mixture of joy and melancholy. She wanted nothing more than to leap at Cate and cover her with kisses. But every time she thought of stroking her hands over Cate's body the image and sensation of Rafe intruded. His smell, that mix of fresh sweat and musk deodorant, the way his hard and toned body felt. She covered her mouth and gasped with grief. 'Why couldn't you have been single?'

'I know this is an incredible mess,' Cate begged. 'But please give us a chance. If not straight away, then in a little while.'

Pia listened to what Cate said. She tried to entertain the scenario in her head. Her insides swelled with love and warmth whenever she thought of them together. Her heart felt like it might burst with the things Cate had said about loving and adoring her.

But every time, that same chill shivered through her. Visions of Cate walking down the aisle with Rafe, him leading her to the marital bed, their naked bodies entwined in passion.

'I can't.' Pia shook her head, distraught. 'I would think of you with Rafe all the time. And if not Rafe, there would be the fear of someone else.'

Cate looked shocked and hurt.

'I'd put any thought of being with you out of my mind.' Pia said, 'I thought that I was nothing to you. I was happy in a way, being the used other woman and being a bit righteous. But I don't know how to cope with this. I don't think I can cope with this.'

'Please Pia. Don't write us off straight away.' Cate clasped Pia's hands. 'God I know this is a terrible start. But I have never felt this way about someone. Please don't give up.'

Pia stood, shaking, and wrapped her clothes around her. 'I'm sorry. I don't know how to get over it.' She edged away, barefoot in her trousers and shirt. Her heart was filled with the unbearable mix of loving someone she couldn't abide to be with.

'Pia please,' Cate called to her.

Heart-stopping grief had plunged deep inside and Pia couldn't speak. She kept walking.

'I will wait for you,' was the last thing she heard Cate say.

23

Pia sloped through the front door, her shoes still untied and her jacket over her arm.

Her mother peeped over a newspaper, and her face sank into sympathy as soon as she saw Pia's dejection. 'Oh no.' She folded her paper away and waved her forward. 'Come on. Come tell Mama everything.'

Pia shuffled over, her mouth twitching down, and she started to blub. She dropped to her knees and buried her face into her mother's lap.

'Oh dear. Oh dear.' Her mama held her head and rocked her back and forth.

Pia talked into her mother's dress through a stream of dribble. 'She said she loved me, Mama. She said she wanted to be together.'

Her mother stroked her hair. 'It doesn't surprise me. Doesn't surprise me at all.'

Pia broke into another sob, assuming her mother would be as surprised as she. She stifled her sniffles as her mother's actual reaction sank in.

'Really?'

Her mother held her face. 'Oh, don't give me those big hopeless eyes. Of course it doesn't surprise me. You are a beautiful, adorable girl. Why wouldn't she want you?'

'Because she's incredible, Mama. She is beautiful, clever, interesting and funny when I least expect it. She makes my heart beat like crazy even when she sips lemonade. She has that magic and…' Pia realised with surprise that the thing that warmed her through and through was that she enjoyed her company. 'I just like her. I love her. I adore her. But most of all I like her.'

In that second she saw scenes of happiness: Making breakfast at the weekend with the morning sun streaming through the window; lying in the garden reading the paper; squeezing Cate's sore feet at the end of a long day.

She stared at her mother in shock before her lips gave in to another spasm of misery. 'It's such a mess.' And she buried her head in her hands.

'Oh mija. Of course it's a mess. She's married. What else did you think it would be?'

'But it's not fair.' Pia sniffled. 'Why do I have to meet the perfect woman on the night before her wedding?'

'Now Pia.' She took Pia's hands away from her face. 'Listen to what you're saying. You, miss picky pants, miss there's nothing special about the several millions of girls in London. You have met someone you think is perfect. That's fantastico.'

'But it's impossible.'

'Why?'

'I can't help thinking about her with Rafe. Our night was so special. I was blown away by her and I thought she felt the same. If she can jump into bed with someone else after that, how could I trust her in the future? When things might not be going so well. What would she do?'

Her mother shrugged. 'You do have a point. But life's like that. Never easy. Never predictable.'

Pia breathed out in frustration. 'Why can't I find love like you and Dad?'

'Oh see, now you talk rubbish.' Her mother threw up her arms.

'But you and Dad had the most perfect romance. Love at first sight. Dad pursuing you. Eloping.'

'And now? What do you see? Your dad is in prison. We scrape by with the rent every month. I'm lonely, with only a sniffling daughter for company.'

Pia felt a little ashamed.

'But I would not change a thing,' her mother said with a warm smile. 'I still love your papa. Is it always easy? No. He's the most annoying man in the world. He's drives me crazy. Things get messy and it's hard. That's what real love's about. If you want the love of your life, then you have to put up with some real life too.'

Pia looked away, wishing she could be as pragmatic as her mother. 'I love her, Mama. I've never loved anyone like this. But it doesn't feel right. I can't cope with how it's started. It's all gone too wrong.'

Her mother picked up her hands. 'Come on. You're usually the one to see the diamond in the cowpat. Now all you see is cowpat. You need someone to come along and rinse off that diamond. Then you can admire the diamond, still see the cowpat, but not step in the shit, heh?'

Pia hung her head down. 'I hope so, Mama.'

'How is he?' Cate asked.

Wynne's voice sounded concerned on the other end of the telephone. 'Much the same I'm afraid. They'll keep him in at least overnight.'

'Is he talking?'

'Just garbage. You know, more than usual.' A twinge of sadness squeezed Cate's chest at her grandmother's making light, even at her most anxious.

'Would you mind helping Wilkins?' Lady Wynne continued. 'Make sure he has everything he needs to bring the party to a close.'

'Of course. Most people left straight away and send their best wishes.' Cate glanced round. There were a few stragglers. They chatted in sparse groups in the harsh full lights of the ballroom. The jazz band shuffled at the back and packed away their instruments. 'Are you going to stay in overnight too?'

'If I can. Will you be all right there by yourself?'

'Yes, but would you like me to keep you company in the hospital?'

'No, I'm fine. Thank you darling. Get a good night's sleep. It looks like I will need your help in the morning. Good night sweetheart.'

'Good night.'

Cate stroked her finger across the screen and stared at the phone. It trembled in her hands. Her arms were light with fatigue and shock. She shivered, trying to rekindle her energy.

'Ma'am?'

Cate twirled round to see Wilkins. 'Please, call me Catherine.'

He nodded.

'How can I help?' Cate asked.

'The caterers hadn't served food and most of it's still chilled in their van. They were wondering whether it should be stored in the kitchen.'

'Oh.' Cate shook her head. Lucid thought was difficult. 'Could you make sure the staff have been fed and then tell the caterers to donate the rest to the food charity?'

Wilkins nodded and took his leave.

Cate cradled her phone to her chest and peered around the ballroom. Her heart sank at the prospect of polite chitchat with the lingering guests. She straightened her spine and pushed back her shoulders. She attempted a gracious smile, but that failed her tonight.

Playing the polite hostess, she engaged every last guest in conversation, placating the anxieties of even the most inquisitive and intrusive. She escorted couple after couple to the hall doors, nodding at looks and words of cloying sympathy, and kissed the partygoers farewell.

When the last chauffeur-driven car crunched along the driveway, she closed the great doors and the sound echoed around the hall.

Wilkins strode towards her. 'The caterers have cleared out the kitchen and ballroom, although they still need to finish cleaning.'

Cate raised her hand. 'Let's worry about that in the morning. Send everyone home please. You turn in too.'

Wilkins gave a sharp nod. 'Good night ma'am.' And he withdrew to the kitchens.

Cate's heels were harsh on the empty floor. She made her way to the ballroom, every step that bit heavier and slower. She stood in the large double doorway. The band had cleared, the guests had gone. All that was left were the marks of hundreds of footfalls and the odd serviette dropped on the floor. She reached round to the panel of old metal light switches. She clunked them down one at a time, a slice of ballroom disappearing into the darkness with each. When the last one was extinguished, she leant back against the wall, hidden from view.

Her legs gave way and she sank to the floor. She buried her face in her hands and started to sob into her knees. While a hot tear seeped through her eyelashes and tickled wet down her cheek, her mind's eye saw Pia leaving, distraught.

It was impossible not to look back and search for all the times when she could have stopped all the hurt. She remembered the wedding day. She stood in the archway and stared down the flower-lined aisle to Rafe. Hundreds of guests watched her as she stood alone at the end of the walkway. Rafe turned around, a look of pride on his face. She hesitated. She didn't know if anyone else noticed, but he did. His face contorted with irritation and his shoulders twitched. She saw his lips move around the words 'Come on now'.

She realised, as she remembered taking that heavy step forward, that that had been her last chance of happiness. And how she wished, for everyone's sake, that she had walked away.

24

Pia stepped into the office with more than a little trepidation on Monday morning. She dreaded seeing Cate, and Rafe more so. But the entire mood of the building was grim. Denise on reception only managed half a smile when Pia bid her good morning.

Ed stuck her head out of her office and beckoned her in without a word.

'Close the door shortarse,' she said, subdued.

Ed sat with her feet on the desk and arms across her chest. She sighed long and hard. 'Cate's not coming in, and I suspect she won't again.'

'Oh.' A strange mix of relief and sadness mixed in Pia's belly. 'What's up?'

Ed tilted her head to the side and raised her eyebrows. 'Well, would you believe it, her grandfather is quite ill from a blow to the head.'

'What? I thought he was going to be OK.'

Ed raised her palms. 'It's all right. He's not fighting for his life or anything critical like that. But he's having one or two difficulties.'

A cold feeling of nausea swirled inside Pia.

'I imagine there are post-concussion complications,' Ed said. 'Maybe it knocked some sense into the old bugger.'

Pia glanced up to see a slight smile on Ed's lips.

'I think it's an excuse more than anything,' Ed continued. 'She's helping Lady Wynne to take care of Charles and sort out all the business that he attends to. But I also think the timing is fortuitous and I doubt Cate will return to the office.'

Pia gulped, unable to restrain her curiosity. 'Have you talked to her?'

'I have.'

'Is she OK?'

Ed leaned over her desk and peered deep into Pia's eyes as if she could see every naughty thing she'd ever done. 'No she's not OK shortarse. What the hell do you think you're doing?'

Pia groaned. 'Oh no, not you too?'

Ed chuckled. 'Has someone been bending your ear?'

Pia nodded. 'My mama.'

'Ha! Good woman. Did she say that you were a hopeless bloody romantic and needed to grow up?'

Pia opened her mouth, shocked. 'No. She was a lot nicer.'

'Really?' Ed seemed perplexed. She shook her head. 'Bloody good job I didn't have kids then. However, Pia Benitez-Smith, you're a hopeless bloody romantic; now grow up. Cate is an incredible lady. One who has integrity, high standards, a moral compass. Fucking annoying in a journalist, but I thought she would be perfect for someone like you who admires such things. You've had this earth-shattering love for her, and now that she's bravely sorting out her life you've decided you're a bit squeamish about how you met and the slight matter of her involvement with a man, that if you'd had a half a brain to ask about you would have avoided in the first place.'

Pia stared at Ed. 'Mama didn't say that either.'

'Well somebody bloody had to.'

Pia looked down at her hands folded and dejected in her lap.

'Shortarse.' Ed was more conciliatory. 'Are you going to walk away from someone who is probably the love of your life?'

'I wish I could get over it. My head says to forgive and try again. I know I'm the luckiest person alive to have someone like Cate love me. But my heart still hurts and I can't do what it doesn't want to.'

Ed sat back and puffed out. 'Jesus. I could knock your heads together. I really could.' She inhaled through her nose and leaned forward again. 'I do understand shortarse. I hope you don't regret it, that's all.'

—

Work seemed an empty place without Cate. Pia rattled around London doing Ed's bidding, but the excitement, the real joy, she realised had gone. She took photos that were adequate, some even good. Ed complimented her at times, but she realised how important Cate's approval had been to her now that she wasn't there. The shine of working for the gossip magazine was tarnished and the motivation to get that one exceptional image was gone.

Every day she peeped at the contacts icon on her phone. It took every bit of will power not to tap through to Cate's name. The temptation to send a simple text and be with Cate via a few simple characters was overwhelming.

Pia loitered in the corridor of the office one morning practising just this masochism when her fingers refused her bidding and stroked through to her number. She was shocked when her phone started to connect.

'You all right mate?' Rafe's voice came so clear from his office that Pia thought he was speaking to her. She snapped her thumb over her phone to end the call and scrambled it into her pocket.

Rafe's door was ajar, the key in the lock as always, but he remained inside.

'Yeah yeah,' he said. 'Doesn't take long for gossip to get round does it?'

Pia tip-toed forward to peek inside the room. Rafe sat with his feet on the large desk, glass of whisky in hand and phone cradled between his shoulder and ear. His hair was flat and a day or two of stubble peppered his chin. But his voice still had his customary bravado.

'Yeah, the fucking bitch. I couldn't believe it. You wouldn't believe the shit I've had to put up with.'

Pia froze at his harsh words that could only have been aimed at Cate.

'Still gave her a fucking huge white wedding and a honeymoon a hundred women would have killed for.'

Conciliatory words must have been said on the other end of the line.

'Don't worry about me mate. I'll get over the bitch. You shouldn't feel too sorry for me either. It's not as if I haven't been getting my end away.'

Pia heard a tinny male laugh from the phone. Rafe grinned and stared out of the window as his friend talked.

'You know me too well mate. I had her over my desk on the first day here.'

Pia twitched back with revulsion. An instant image appeared in Pia's head of Cate reclined over the desk with Rafe inside her. She turned away with nausea curdling her stomach.

The eavesdropping was a tonic for her temptation and her phone thereafter remained resolutely in her pocket. There was one person, however, that she thought she should see, no matter how unwelcome or unpleasant, and that was Sir Charles.

Pia loitered around the gates to the mansion one morning until she saw Cate drive out in Lady Wynne's Jaguar. She was escorted by the butler to the large entrance hall where she waited to be seen. It was cool inside the cavernous hall. The sun blazed in the bright green gardens through the windows and Pia gazed in disbelief at the ancestral home of the woman she loved and who loved her.

Her reverie was broken by rapid echoing steps. She sprung to her feet, anxious at Lady Wynne's reaction, and ready to leave if that was appropriate.

Lady Wynne entered from the ballroom, her expression pained and her arms outstretched. 'My darling Pia.' She covered the ground in quick steps and threw her arms around Pia's neck. 'I'm so glad you've come, but you've missed her by seconds.'

'Oh no,' Pia said, flustered. 'I came to see you and Sir Charles.'

Wynne looked disappointed and a little perplexed.

'I wanted to check he was all right.' Pia was timid. 'How is he?'

'You can see for yourself.' She took Pia's arm and led her outside. She pointed her freckled hand towards the lawn where an elderly gentleman lay on the grass.

'Is he OK?'

'Go and see,' Wynne said with a warm smile.

'Are you sure?' Pia was nervous at approaching the gunman and also at how altered she might find him.

'Quite sure my dear.'

Pia edged towards the lawn. He lay so still in the sun. She trod over the grass, alert to any movement. More than a small fear of finding him dead gripped her chest.

Glassy, unblinking eyes stared at the sky. His white, bony fingers were entwined over his heart. For a horrible moment she thought she was going to have to reach out and prod him.

'Hello? Sir?' she whispered.

He blinked, sniffed, coughed a little and came to. He shaded his brow and sat up. 'Hello,' he offered. It was neither a question nor a confident greeting. He regarded her with interest. 'I'm terribly sorry my dear. Not a clue who you are.'

She knelt down and offered a hand. 'It's Pia sir. Pia Benitez-Smith.'

He took her hand in a firm shake, with the vigour of someone who'd been bred to be superior.

'I'm very sorry my dear. Wynne says I should know lots of these people who visit. But I haven't a bloody clue who they are. Pia, did you say?'

She nodded, wondering what memories would surface.

'Spanish name?'

'That's right sir.'

Sir Charles squinted in concentration. 'You remind me of a fellow I used to serve with. Chap called Peter. Handsome devil. Slight chap, but very successful with the ladies. He was very nice fellow with it all too.'

Pia had no idea if this was a true memory, or if she had become garbled with someone else. Sir Charles stared at her and a flicker of recognition flitted across his face. She tried to keep calm while she waited for the penny to drop and a torrent of abuse to start. He tilted his head to one side, his frown intensifying, and she closed her eyes for the inevitable wrath.

'Do you fancy giving me hand?' he said.

She opened one eye and saw the garden. She opened two and saw more garden. She turned around. Sir Charles had walked to the border and was bringing back a fork and spade. He threw the prongs of the fork into the ground by her feet and set to work with the spade.

'Um. Sir?' Pia checked for Lady Wynne but there was no-one in sight. 'What are you doing?'

Sir Charles stopped and stared at her with a disapproving look that was much more like his old self. 'Digging. What the bloody hell does it look like? Are you a half-wit?'

Pia blushed. 'I mean, should you be digging up the lawn?'

'Oh I see.' He stopped and leaned on the spade. 'Well, I was flicking through some books in the library and I found a photo of the old place during the war. The entire east lawn was planted with veg. I thought it the most heartening sight. Britain resisting and feeding itself.' A breath later he asked 'Are you German, Pia?'

'No sir. Spanish. Half Spanish.'

'Yes, you did say didn't you? Can't be helped.' And he started to dig again. 'You know I've had a funny thought.' He peered up. 'Do you know my granddaughter?'

'Yes sir. I do.' Pia wondered if he caught the sorrow in her voice.

'Lovely girl. Intelligent, beautiful and devilish sense of humour at times. I thought the two of you might hit it off.'

'Thank you,' Pia said with a fond smile. 'We used to work together and I liked her very much.'

'Indeed?' He raised an eyebrow and chuckled. 'I thought there'd be a spark or two, if you know what I mean.'

Pia opened her mouth, but no coherent words came out. 'Um. You do realise that I'm a woman sir.'

'Yes,' he said, as if this was obvious. 'Oh, I see what you mean.' He pondered. 'Can't be helped.' He continued to dig and Pia could think of nothing better to do than help the old man dig his vegetable plot.

Later Pia sat under a tree with Lady Wynne. They watched Sir Charles methodically dig rows across the erstwhile pristine lawn.

'He's not quite all there is he?' Pia said.

'No he's not,' replied Wynne. She looked with fondness towards her husband. 'But at least the good bits are.'

'Will he get better?'

Wynne sighed. 'Well depending on your point of view, probably not. But there are advantages to his current state. He's happier for one, and so is everyone else.'

Pia stared at Charles and shook her head. 'I'm so sorry. This is all my fault.'

'Oh, and that silly buffoon wielding a shotgun had nothing to do with it.'

Pia covered her face not wanting to see Lady Wynne's reaction. 'Do you know what happened?'

Lady Wynne's fingers squeezed her arm in reassurance. 'Cate told me everything my dear,' she whispered. 'She's told me everything, right back to when you first met, and I'm very glad the silly old bugger didn't manage to shoot you.'

Pia slipped her hands away and looked at Lady Wynne. She saw kindness and regret in her face.

'Are you sure you don't want to see Cate?' Wynne said.

'I want to see Cate every second of the day.'

—

Lady Wynne watched from an upstairs window. She watched Pia walk away from the house, down the gravel driveway and into the city beyond the walls.

'She's still very hurt.'

Cate nodded, and touched her fingers to the glass. She leant in close to watch Pia until the very last sight of her.

Her grandmother squeezed her shoulder in affection and comfort. 'I think you should go darling. You need to get on with your life. Go to New York and do all those things you dreamt of. I can be your safety net now.'

They both regarded Sir Charles who was tearing up the east lawn.

'And when you divorce Rafe, find someone like Pia and settle down. I promise I will see you right. Pia's done you more than one favour you know.'

They peered down sadly at the new agreeable version of Sir Charles.

'Thank you,' Cate said. 'But there's no-one in the world like Pia.'

25

Monday morning came around again and again. Pia set off to work with half a heart. Even her beloved second-hand Vespa seemed apathetic today. It coughed and spluttered black fumes and gave the distinct impression of being unwell. It whirred over London Bridge and, by the time it reached Fleet Street, disgruntled cyclists overtook her with ungracious glances.

She pulled up in her usual spot and remained seated, reluctant to start another week of being reminded of Cate's absence.

'Come on.' She swung her heavy legs from the scooter and settled her rucksack on her shoulders. Disgruntled and moping, she sighed down at her own feet. Then she stepped onto the pavement and walked straight into an iced coffee.

'Wooargh.'

'Watch out love!' An irate man shouted at her from behind a now empty plastic cup.

Freezing brown liquid soaked into her white T-shirt. It ran its frosty way down into her bra, down her belly and down her trousers, and a small icy drop seeped into her knickers. She shivered and pinched her shirt away from her belly. 'Sorry.'

'Just mind where you're bloody going.' The man marched away with a backwards glare of censure.

Pia looked down at the brown stain from her breasts to her groin. 'OK. So it's going to be that kind of day.'

By checking in every direction on all occasions, the rest of the short journey proved beverage-free. She found a quiet end office, which was inexplicably empty, and dumped her rucksack on the desk. She slumped into the chair, which gave a little, and leaned against its back, which gave a lot. It was so giving in fact that it collapsed and flipped her over.

'What the…?'

She lay on the floor, her legs hooked over the upturned seat. As she gazed up at her shoes and brown stained groin, she contemplated whether this was the reason for the office's lack of occupancy. In any case, she decided it might be best not to move until lunchtime.

Her phone buzzed in her pocket and, having very little else to occupy her on the floor, she answered it.

'Hi.'

Pia's heart leapt at the sound of Cate's greeting. She took a few moments to respond, struck dumb by Cate's beautiful voice, sudden and vivid. 'Hi,' she managed.

'I wasn't sure you'd answer.' Cate sounded melancholy. 'How are you?'

'I'm…I'm fine thank you.'

'You sound rough. Do you have a cold?'

Pia sounded nasal on her back with her feet in the air. 'I'm just lying around.'

They were silent for a few moments. It could have been minutes.

'I wanted to talk to you before I left. I'm going to Paris for a few days. I'm helping cover the election. Then I'm going to New York.'

'The secondment to the *New York Times*?' Pia forgot herself in her excitement for Cate. She tried to sit up but realised she would need to do a backward somersault to extract herself from between the desk, chair and wall.

'Yes. I called them on the off chance, and they still wanted me to join.' Cate hesitated. 'I've signed a two-year contract.'

It knocked the last bit of joy out of Pia. It had a finality that hurt even though Pia knew they couldn't be together. She tried to smile, to be happy for Cate.

'I hope it's as good as your dreams.' Pia closed her eyes in despair when she remembered what Cate's dream had been. The thought that she would find someone in New York to cherish and love and hold at night cut like a knife through her heart.

They were silent again. In the background she heard someone, perhaps Lady Wynne, whisper 'Darling, we'd better set off for the station.'

Cate's reply was indistinct but then: 'Pia?'

'I'd better go anyway.' The image of Cate happy with someone else had made Pia choke.

'Ring me,' Cate said quietly. 'Day or night. Ring me if you want to talk.'

Pia nodded, gulping down a sob.

'Are you OK?'

Pia sniffed, 'Only a cold.'

'I thought you said you were all right.'

'Came on suddenly. Better go. Good luck.' And Pia fumbled to end the call.

She lay on the floor, utterly despondent, the cold, brown coffee stain clinging to her tummy. There she stayed for some unknown time until Ed's face appeared in the air above. Ed's expression of concern changed to bemusement with the twitch of an eyebrow.

'Hi Ed,' Pia said, deflated. 'Please don't ask.'

'Are things that bad? You know throwing yourself off a chair is no way to end it all.'

Pia lightened with a fraction of a mental smile. 'Just shoot me.'

'Well people have tried my dear.' Ed grinned. 'But before we ring Sir Charles for another attempt on your life, you have a visitor in reception.'

'I'm not expecting anyone.'

'Not an attractive Spanish lady?'

Perplexed, Pia extricated herself from the chair and wall using an inelegant manoeuvre and followed Ed to the door. Ed peeped into the corridor with a keen look on her face.

'Ed. That's my mama!' Ed was quite obviously admiring her.

'Really?' Ed took another appreciative glance. 'Well, congratulations on superior genes missy. You are going to be a scorcher in middle age.' Ed raised her hand to quash any further objections and disappeared with a smirk before Pia could retaliate.

The reception area was empty and Denise was absent from the desk. Her mama was free to stride around admiring the large Bennet sign and posters from the first edition that decorated the walls. She lingered by the spread of Cate's article and Pia's photo of the London Fashion Show. Pia's heart swelled when she saw her mother clasp her hands together in pride.

'Hi Mama.' Pia smiled, the first proper feeling of cheer she'd had all day.

'Pia. My little Pia.' She came towards her, arms open with proud delight. She drew her close but with a second thought pushed her away. She scanned Pia's front.

'Oh mija. What do you do on the way to work?'

'I had an unlucky morning.'

'Oh come here anyway.' And her mother smothered her with an embrace.

'What are you doing here, Mama?' Pia said, half strangled and half delighted.

'I thought I'd come to see where my lovely, talented daughter works.' She rocked her from side to side. 'And I thought you seemed very down so I wonder if you fancy some lunch today.'

Pia pulled back. 'I shouldn't today. I've made such a slow start.'

Her mother tried to cover her disappointment with an understanding smile, but it was enough for Pia to regret her refusal. 'How about you stay for a coffee though?' she offered. 'I can show you around and you can meet Ed.'

Her mother's beaming grin was her acceptance.

—

'Sit here, Mama.' Pia patted a chair by the kitchen window with a splendid view of Fleet Street below. She searched through the empty cupboards. 'We're out of coffee, and I don't know where Denise keeps it. I'll be back in a minute.'

She poked her head around the corner but the reception area was still empty. Pia walked through the offices, none with any sign of Denise. She was about to press the bell on the reception desk when the storeroom door opened. A giggling Denise tripped out, pinching her hair back into place. She was followed by Rafe, whose rosy cheeks and the fumbling with his fly left little to the imagination.

Pia blushed and turned up the corridor.

'Shit,' she heard Denise say. Rafe shouted, 'Pia. Wait.'

His feet pounded along the floor behind her and he grabbed her by the arm. She tried to snatch it away but he forced her into his office. She fumed, indignant that Rafe had moved on so swiftly from Cate. It was galling that the man who'd kept them apart showed so little grief.

'Rafe, it's none of my business. I'm trying to find some coffee.'

She turned to leave but Rafe dragged her round to within a few inches of his face. His eyes were unfocussed and his breath stank of alcohol, which in all likelihood contributed to his rosy complexion as much as any activity in the storeroom with Denise.

'Please don't tell anyone,' he slurred. 'I don't want people thinking I'm a shit.'

Pia tried to swallow away her distaste but repulsion still rippled her features. 'Really Rafe, I don't care and I won't tell anyone. I have to get back to Mama.'

'It's over with Cate.' He looked earnest. 'I know you got on well and I want you to understand I'm not being unfaithful to her or anything.'

'I'm sorry to hear it's over. Please, I have to go.'

Rafe pawed at her. 'You have to believe me. That's the first time anything's happened.'

Pia thought back to the karaoke at Rafe's house and Denise's inclination towards him. The liaison no longer surprised her and she stiffened with irritation that here was another person so fickle with their love.

'Well that's great. I hope you'll be happy if that's what you both want.'

'Listen,' he slurred. 'Actually it's not the first time.' His head drooped with obvious guilt. 'Please don't tell anyone.'

'I won't. I don't even talk to Cate anymore.'

'She's the one who left me. It was over before it started. Could you tell? Could you all bloody tell?'

'No,' Pia muttered, mindful of Rafe's temper.

'Did I look like a fucking fool parading her around?' His chin jutted with wounded pride.

'Rafe, I didn't notice anything.'

'It was obvious though.' His face flushed and his voice trembled with angry bitterness.

'You made a handsome couple.' Pia wanted to placate him, although imagining them together made her feel ill.

'I was stupid,' he spat. 'She didn't want to get married. I should have let the bitch go.'

Pia was about to console him once again when she hesitated. 'What did you say?' A small involuntary spark of

216

hope ignited within her, but she wasn't sure that she'd heard correctly. She waited, trying to dampen down a rising sense of optimism. 'What did you say, Rafe?'

'I had to beg her to marry me.' His lips curled in disgust. 'It was fucking humiliating. Begging the woman I loved and who was meant to love me.'

'When? When was this?'

'On the morning of the wedding. The actual fucking morning. Can you believe it? She disappeared on her hen night. No-one knows where she went. She turned up in the morning and said she couldn't go through with it.'

Fear chilled and numbed Pia's limbs, while hope glimmered deep inside.

'She said she met someone. On her fucking hen night. She said she couldn't go through with it. That she didn't feel the right way about me and she wasn't being fair. I pleaded with her to stay. I told her it was stupid to leave for someone she'd just met. We had five hundred fucking guests waiting for us. I didn't want to go out to tell them all.'

Pia stared at him.

'Do you know the only sex I've had as married man has been with Denise? How fucking crap is that?'

A smile burst across Pia's face. She gasped and covered her mouth. The hope that had glimmered now shone and she was filled with sudden joy. Cate hadn't been able to consummate their marriage. She hadn't been able to sleep with Rafe after meeting her.

He shook his head. 'I haven't been able to touch her. She'd hardly come near me.'

'I'm sorry,' Pia blurted out.

Rafe lifted his head up, his cheeks still full-blooded with anger. 'Why are you sorry? It's not your bloody fault.'

Pia opened her mouth but no words came.

'What's wrong?' he said. 'What do you know?'

She was breathing hard, unable to control her fear or the swell of love for Cate that filled her chest. 'It was me.' Her voice shook.

'What? What did you say?'

'She met me that night.'

It took several seconds for it to register at all. Then he shook his head in disbelief. 'You? What would she be doing with you?'

'We met in passing. It was a coincidence. I was near her flat when she left for the party.'

'And? What?' Incredulity was heavy in his voice, 'You fell into bed by accident?'

'Oh God. I'm sorry, Rafe. I'm in love with her and I have to go.'

She backed away. Rafe's eyes never left hers, his expression still stupid with surprise.

As she reached the doorway, Rafe's face darkened with fury. 'You're not fucking kidding are you? You're telling me the truth.'

He started towards her. He swayed, uncoordinated with alcohol, but his angry energy carried him forward. 'I don't fucking believe it. It was you!'

Pia stumbled back, grabbing for the door handle.

'You fucking bitch. You fucking lezzer!'

With a swift and terrified movement Pia slammed the door shut and clicked the key in the lock. Rafe's fists pounded on the door. His yell was muffled but his desperate kicks reverberated around the office.

'Open the door you fucking bitch!'

Pia stared at the door, her heart pounding with adrenaline, fear and love.

26

In an instant, Pia's image of Cate changed. She was irresistible. Her warm smile. A flash of mischief in her eyes when she caught Pia unaware. The sensual curve of her body and the addictive allure of her soft skin, receptive only to Pia's touch.

She remembered how adamant Cate had been when she promised she would be faithful to Pia. How hollow it had seemed when all Pia could imagine was Cate in Rafe's arms.

'Oh God.' Pia put her hands to her face.

How badly she'd under-estimated her. How insensitive she'd been dismissing Cate's depth of feeling for her.

'Shit, shit, shit!' She stumbled back into the corridor and straight into the bosoms of Ed and her mother.

'You all right shortarse? You look as if you've seen the second coming.'

'Ed, I've fucked up.'

'In what way dear? The times are too numerous to count.'

'Open the fucking door, Pia!' Rafe hammered his fists on the wall.

'Ah.' Ed flicked her gaze towards the door. 'This would be about Cate then.'

Pia's throat was too constricted with emotion to speak and she nodded.

'I suppose he knows about your romantic interlude before his wedding?'

'Pia!' Rafe growled and he kicked the door with such force the office wall began to move.

Ed led them down the corridor to a quieter spot. 'Tell me, what's happened?'

'I've really, really fucked up.'

'Well we all know that dear.'

Pia appealed to her mother who stood close, but she shrugged in agreement.

'She loves me,' Pia said. 'She loved me all along. But I didn't give her time. Why didn't I listen to her?'

Ed looked up in thought and suggested, 'Pride, youthful stubbornness, naivete?' She glared back at Pia. 'You're absurdly romantic, and frankly judgemental at times. Then there's plain stupidity—'

'OK. OK. I said I fucked up. But what am I going to do?'

'Talk to her, mija.' Her mother regarded Pia with a mix of sympathy, exasperation and tearful joy. 'You need to talk to Cate.'

'Well there's an idea shortarse.' Ed rolled her eyes.

'But…shit.' Pia snatched out her phone. She had no idea what she was going to say. But she really did need to talk to Cate now.

She tapped through to the last caller and listened to the silence of her phone attempting to connect. All she could hear was her own rasping breath, her heaving heartbeat pulsing in her ears and Rafe pounding the door.

A piercing beep broke the silence. 'It's engaged.' Pia's voice was strident. 'She's leaving for Paris and New York today. I think she's already at the station.'

'Calm down a minute.' Ed took her by the arms. 'Before you do anything absurd like running off to St Pancras station, are you sure you can do this? Can you love Cate after she married Rafe? With no reservations? No ifs, no buts, no recriminations of "this is just like that time you ran off with a minor royal"?'

'Yes I can. It was over before it started. She hasn't slept with him since the wedding. I should have seen it. It was written all over her face. Her head chose Rafe but her heart chose me.'

'Hmm.' Ed rubbed her chin. 'Well oh dear.'

Pia's mother came close and hugged Pia round her shoulders.

'So she did want you all along?' Ed sounded grave.

'Yes.'

'And you slept with her. Then said you never wanted to see her again?'

'It wasn't…I didn't…Basically…Yes.' Pia covered her face. Any jubilation she'd felt evaporated in despair.

'And you've blown it so completely that she's moving to a different continent.'

'Oh God.'

'There's no way Cate would give you a chance now.'

Pia moaned distraught.

'Not a prayer she'd want the woman she can never take her eyes off.'

Pia peeped through her fingers, choking with sadness, but also a little puzzled.

Ed grinned. 'Nothing in the world would persuade her to take someone who gives her the same joy and amazement as seeing the first bloody sunrise.'

Pia's mood began to lift. She looked to her mother.

'Go on mija. Go get her.'

Pia swirled round but hesitated. 'What about Rafe?'

'Who gives a bunch of flying bloody monkeys about Rafe.' Ed shouted. 'Go!'

Pia patted her jeans pocket for her keys and ran down the corridor. The last she heard was Ed bellowing, 'And for Christ's sake don't change your mind on the way.'

—

221

Pia clattered down the stairs. She skidded around the corners as she clung to the bannister. She burst into the street and sprinted to the bike rack. She lobbed on her helmet in a slick, well-practised movement, jumped on her Vespa, turned the ignition and scooted onto Fleet Street. And as she pulled into the main road, she remembered her ailing ride.

'Oh come on!' Her heart sank as the Vespa spluttered to a top speed of ten miles an hour. 'Not today.'

Taxis, buses, cyclists hurtled by. It wouldn't have surprised her if a pedestrian or two had overtaken her. She felt absurd gripping the handle bars tight with desperation as she whirred along in slow motion. Halfway along Farringdon Road, clouds of black fumes coughed out of the scooter's rear. With a loud bang from the exhaust pipe and a whimper from the engine, her bike took its last breath.

Pia leapt off and pushed the heavy bike to the side of the road. For a moment she worried about securing it. Then she wished any joyrider luck and abandoned her helmet and old Vespa. She checked up and down the street trying to remember where the nearest Tube was. All she could see were houses, offices and the security gates to the Mount Pleasant mail centre.

She ran into the kiosk, red-faced, brown-chested and unable to speak. A security guard peered at her, amused, over his tabloid.

'You all right love?'

'Nearest Tube?' she gasped.

'No underground here mate, sorry. It's at least half a mile to the nearest.'

'Where?'

'Right then. To the west, you've got Russell Square.'

Pia turned to look out of the window expecting directions to follow.

'To the south you've got Chancery Lane and Farringdon,' the security guard continued. 'Barbican's another option. Or Holborn come to think of it.'

'Which. Is. Nearest?'

'None of them are particularly handy.' The security guard laughed.

Starting to cross the divide between desperation and insanity, Pia grabbed his paper and snapped, 'How the bloody hell do I get to St Pancras?'

'Well, you should have said love.' He chortled. I'd run up the road. It's as close as the Tube stations.'

'Thank you,' Pia growled and she turned to leave.

'You might want to follow the diversion signs.'

She threw the guard an irritated glance.

'Road's blocked.'

'I'm sure I'll find a way through. Thanks,' she said through gritted teeth.

'If you say so,' was the last she heard before she hurtled up the street.

Pia threw back her head and forced her legs on. Her lungs were raw and her thighs screamed. All the while she chanted in her head. 'Diversion signs. Bloody diversion signs.' Why would she follow diversion signs on foot?

She scurried along the curving pavement where it changed to the King's Cross Road and bid adieu to the traffic that dutifully followed the black on yellow arrows a different route.

And then she saw it. A great lake where the road should be. Brown opaque water rippling across her direct path.

'No. No. No!' She slapped her hands to her head. 'How can this be flooded in the middle of bloody summer?'

She approached the water's edge. It was impossible to see how deep it was. She pushed her toe towards it.

'I wouldn't love,' a voice from above said. She peered up to see the silhouette of a woman three floors up leaning out of a window. 'It's a burst water main, but I'd hate to think what it's mixed up with to be that colour. Just earth they says. Don't believe a word of it.'

Pia shaded her eyes and took a deep breath to shout. 'Do you know where I can get through?'

'It's all over the next couple of streets. I reckon, your best bet, you know, is probably to follow—'

'The diversion signs,' Pia sighed. She shouted her thanks and waved her hand in the air before sprinting on her way breathing, 'Bloody diversion signs.'

—

Pia was doubled over wheezing when, at last, the imposing gothic red towers of St Pancras rose above her. She clasped her side to rub the stitch that pinched there and jogged the last hundred metres. She lurched along, cursing every ornate arched window of the long railway station walls.

She was stumbling into the entrance when a Mini pulled up in the taxi rank. She was amused and confused to see Ed and her mother squashed inside. They burst out as the small doors opened.

'What are you waiting for?' Ed shouted. 'Get inside.' And she waved her on.

Pia's face blazed from exertion as she jogged into the cathedral of St Pancras. The vast iron arches supported a cavernous space and Pia's hope soon turned to defeat at finding Cate in such a vast place.

Panic set in and she dashed along an arcade of shops, towards signs that looked like train details. She scanned notices and realised they were all domestic lines and spun round in a state of mind approaching hysteria.

'Where the hell's Eurostar?' she yelled.

Her answer was quick. Ed and her mother appeared around the corner and gesticulated back in the direction she'd just come from.

'Lounge is this way,' Ed yelled.

She was about to follow when she thought she heard something. She edged around and peered up to the mezzanine. Well-dressed passengers sat in booths along the length of the Champagne bar. Businesspeople huddled around laptops. A group of young women giggled over bubbling glasses. But one figure stared out. Pia's heart tripped over a beat as she caught sight of Cate's beautiful face, still and clear in the blur of the crowd.

Pia started to raise her hand to catch Cate's eye, but Cate's direct look speared her to the spot. Pia froze, fearful of her reaction. Cate seemed shocked, but her face began to twitch. Amusement curled at her lips and rose up her face. Hope sparkled in her eyes.

Cate checked towards the Champagne bar, where Lady Wynne sat, before walking along the balcony. Pia silently watched her all the way to the top of the escalator, and didn't blink as she glided down to her level.

Pia's mouth was still open when Cate stopped a foot away.

'Pia Benitez-Smith,' she said in that silky voice that caressed Pia inside. She smiled down at her shirt. 'How is your day?'

Pia couldn't speak.

Cate reached out with tentative fingers to hold Pia's hand. She gazed into her eyes. 'I'm hoping you're not here by accident,' she said gently.

Pia shook her head, still unable to speak.

'Do we have a chance?' Cate was almost shy.

'Please,' Pia blurted out. 'I'm so sorry.'

'Why are you sorry?'

'Because I never even said I love you, and I haven't thought of anything other than loving you since we met.'

Cate looked at her, worried. 'Can you forgive me?' She drew closer to Pia. 'For not making the right choice at the

225

right time? There wasn't anybody except you since that day.'

'I know that now.' Pia leaned in. The warmth and closeness of Cate made her feel dizzy.

'I love you Pia,' Cate whispered.

Pia felt the words stroke her lips in a breath. Dazed with enchantment she let her head fall into the slight gap between Cate and her.

Cate caught her fall. Their soft lips met in an exquisite touch. Pia closed her eyes and was aware of only where their two bodies met, their lips tingling as they kissed. The feeling glowed all the way to her core. Her body was light with happiness, as if she might float away should Cate let her go. Their lips drifted apart without Pia realising, and it took Cate's fingers stroking her cheek to revive her.

Pia gulped. 'What are we going to do?'

Cate smiled at her, pure uncomplicated love in her expression. 'Come with me. Just come with me.' A glint of excitement sparkled in her expression.

'How can I?'

Cate squeezed her hands. 'Come with me to Paris. We'll get a tourist visa to New York and we can work things out from there. Can you leave the magazine?'

Pia was sheepish. 'I think I might have been sacked. But I still need a passport.' Her shoulders fell despondent. The thought of having to spend another second away from Cate was painful.

She heard a cough and turned round. Ed, her mother and Lady Wynne, who had descended from the Champagne bar, were all watching from a short distance. And her mother was waving a passport in the air.

'We nipped home. Just in case.' Her mama grinned.

Pia glanced down at her dirty T-shirt and stained jeans. 'I need to get something to wear though. How long until the train?'

Her mother gave her a satisfied smile. 'I thought of that too.' She walked towards her holding out a small rucksack. 'Enough for you to elope with, and I should know.'

She handed over the bag and kissed Pia on the cheek. As she stepped back she addressed Cate. 'Take care of her. She needs it sometimes.'

'Oh Mama. Is this OK?'

'Of course.' She clasped her hands together. 'I couldn't wish for anything better for my Pia.'

Cate touched her arm. 'I'm so sorry. We need to hurry though.'

Pia held Cate's hand and peeped over her shoulder one last time to see Ed, Wynne and her mother all waving them goodbye. They started to walk and she turned to Cate, apprehensive.

She saw the same look of nervous excitement in her eyes. Cate grinned, unreserved happiness on her face and Pia caught her infectious joy. She laughed as they ran under the great sky of St Pancras swinging their hands together.

###

Acknowledgements

I'm very grateful for the help and patience of some very good people.

Most patient of all was Jayne Fereday through relentless rereads and grilling for feedback and she also tarted up the final version. As well as being an ex-rocket scientist and a copyeditor she also does a mean book cover.

Extended family Fereday should also be thanked. Pat and Roger provided baby-sitting duties which allowed valuable writing time, otherwise this novel would have taken a decade to write. They also supplied artwork for the lovely cover.

I want to thank Kiki Archer for being that super positive soul and getting me back on track when I needed it. Cindy Rizzo for spotting some nasty slips and giving valuable New Yorker insight. And Eileen Taylor for being a willing and encouraging early reader with essential feedback.

I'm especially grateful to Chris Paynter whose comments have greatly helped me to polish later drafts, and to whom I should apologise for excessive adverbs in this sentence (adverbage?). And Diana Simmonds who suffered the early drafts and last-minute polishing with typical good humour and spot-on advice – yes axe-wielding isn't great foreplay now I come to think of it. These are two great writers whose influence on this novel is obvious.

All remaining issues are my own.

And Jayne, Ellie and Joe, I promise this is the last book. After just the next one, because I have this really good idea…

About the Author

Clare Ashton's first novel, *Pennance*, was long-listed for the Polari Prize and *After Mrs Hamilton* is a Golden Crown Literary Society award winner.

Clare grew up in Mid-Wales and lives in Birmingham with her partner, Jayne, and their two children, Joe and Ellie, who are a lovely distraction from writing. She has a brain stuck somewhere not particularly useful between the arts and science. And that's how she ended up studying History and Philosophy of Science at Cambridge. Before being a mum and writer she worked as a scientific copyeditor (where she learnt to spell diarrhoea), a waitress at the Little Chef (where she learnt you could survive on toast alone) and as a software engineer (where she learnt to spend far too much time on a computer).

She is sometimes accused of living too much inside her head, but it turns out that this is good for writing stories. Her novels are a mix of suspense, romance, humour and darker elements too.

She also edits the UK lesbian fiction blog with Cari Hunter: http://uklesfic.wordpress.com

Also by Clare Ashton
Pennance
After Mrs Hamilton
The Dildo in the Kitchen Drawer

Find out more about Clare
http://rclareashton.wordpress.com
twitter: rclareashton
https://www.facebook.com/pages/Clare-Ashton/327713437267566

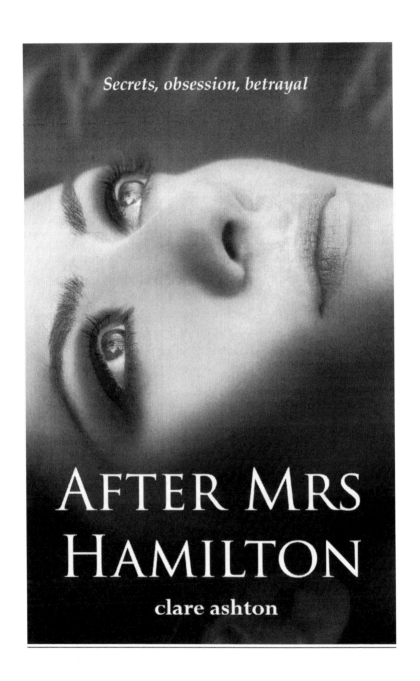

Secrets, obsession, betrayal

AFTER MRS HAMILTON

clare ashton

be careful who you love

PENNANCE

clare
ashton

'a brilliant love story / mystery, beautifully written'
T.T. Thomas